"Why don't I call you later?"
Jared asked.

Katie's stomach did a flip-flop. Was he asking her out? For real?

"I'll sketch out a few ideas for you, then take a look at my calendar and see when I can get started."

Katie nodded, trying hard to mask her disappointment. Though why she'd be disappointed Jared didn't plan to call for a date confused her.

Okay, he was a nice guy. But Katie wasn't exactly looking for a relationship. At least nothing more than a casual partner to accompany her to the town's fireworks display on the Fourth. Someone who'd watch the Super Bowl with her without making comments about how women didn't get football. Especially since she loved the sport.

Surely she didn't have the hots for Jared, did she? She hadn't *really* wanted him to say he'd be calling for a date, had she?

No way.

Dear Reader,

In this season of giving thanks, there's only one thing as good as gathering with your family around the holiday table—this month's Silhouette Romance titles, where you're sure to find everything on your romantic wish list!

Hoping Santa will send you on a trip to sunny climes? Visit the romantic world of La Torchere resort with *Rich Man, Poor Bride* (SR #1742), the second book of the miniseries IN A FAIRY TALE WORLD.... Linda Goodnight brings the magic of matchmaking to life with the tale of a sexy Latino doctor who finds love where he least expects it.

And if you're dreaming of a white Christmas, don't miss Sharon De Vita's *Daddy in the Making* (SR#1743). Here, a love-wary cop and a vivacious single mother find themselves snowbound in Wisconsin. Is that a happily-ever-after waiting for them under the tree?

If you've ever ogled a man in a tool belt, and wanted to make him yours, don't miss *The Bowen Bride* (SR #1744) by Nicole Burnham. This wedding shop owner thinks she'll never wear a bridal gown of her own…until she meets a sexy carpenter and his daughter. Perhaps the next dress she sells will be a perfect fit—for her.

Fill your holiday with laughter, courtesy of a new voice in Silhouette Romance—Nancy Lavo—and her story of a fairy godfather and his charge, in *A Whirlwind…Makeover* (SR #1745). When a celebrity photographer recognizes true beauty beneath this ad exec's bad hair and baggy clothes, he's ready to transform her…but can the armor around his heart withstand the woman she's become?

Here's to having your every holiday wish fulfilled!

Sincerely,

Mavis C. Allen
Associate Senior Editor

Please address questions and book requests to:
Silhouette Reader Service
U.S.: 3010 Walden Ave., P.O. Box 1325, Buffalo, NY 14269
Canadian: P.O. Box 609, Fort Erie, Ont. L2A 5X3

The Bowen Bride

NICOLE BURNHAM

SILHOUETTE *Romance*®

Published by Silhouette Books

America's Publisher of Contemporary Romance

For Joe and Ellen Bull,
my Nebraska grandparents

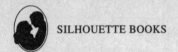 SILHOUETTE BOOKS

ISBN 0-373-19744-6

THE BOWEN BRIDE

Copyright © 2004 by Nicole Burnham Onsi

Visit Silhouette Books at www.eHarlequin.com

Printed in U.S.A.

Books by Nicole Burnham

Silhouette Romance

Going to the Castle #1563
The Prince's Tutor #1640
The Knight's Kiss #1663
One Bachelor To Go #1706
Falling for Prince Federico #1732
The Bowen Bride #1744

*The diTalora Royal Family

NICOLE BURNHAM

is originally from Colorado, but as the daughter of an army dentist grew up traveling the world. She has skied the Swiss Alps, snorkeled in the Grenadines and successfully haggled her way through Cairo's Khan al Khalili marketplace.

After obtaining both a law degree and a master's degree in political science, Nicole settled into what she thought would be a long, secure career as an attorney. That long, secure career only lasted a year—she soon found writing romance a more adventuresome career choice than writing stale legal briefs.

When she's not writing, Nicole enjoys relaxing with her family, tending her rose garden and traveling—the more exotic the locale, the better.

Nicole loves to hear from readers. You can reach her at P.O. Box 229, Hopkinton, MA, 01748-0229, or through her Web site at www.NicoleBurnham.com.

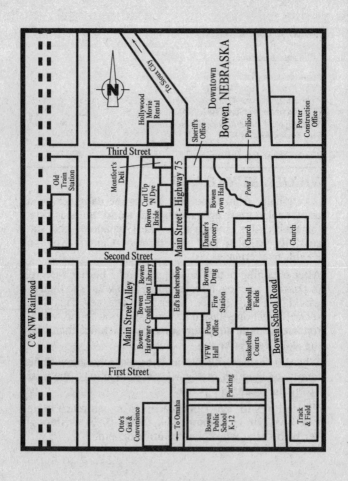

Prologue

"What's with the thread, Oma? You need me to put it away?"

Katie Schmidt watched from beside the bed as her grandmother cradled a brownish, oversize spool between her arthritic fingers, then set it down in her lap as delicately as if it belonged in a museum case.

"No, Katarina." The older woman smiled to herself, then lifted her head to focus clear blue eyes on Katie. "This thread is the story of our family. I had your father get it from my cedar chest for you. You will listen to me now, *ja?* It is very important you listen."

"I'm listening." Katie flashed Oma a smile, then busied herself smoothing the afghan at the foot of Oma's bed. Oma was dying—Katie's father had broken that news to her several months ago—but not of any illness that would affect her thinking.

"Come, *Schatzi*." The gray-haired woman patted a small space near her hip just wide enough for eighteen-year-old Katie to occupy. "I will tell you the truth about this old thread. It has saved our family many times. And now I give it to you. This thread, you see, it is magic."

Katie didn't smirk or roll her eyes, though she knew most of her friends would. From an early age, her father had taught her that Oma deserved serious respect. Oma's grandparents came over from Germany in the late 1800s, along with the rest of Bowen, Nebraska's first settlers, to work for the railroad. Their son, Oma's father, became the town's second— and still most beloved—mayor. The fire station, built during his time in office, still bore a huge plaque with his name.

Oma's mother, whose family emigrated from Germany just before World War I, raised most of the money to build the town's first multiroom school. She'd made certain Oma would be the first person from Bowen, male or female, to attend college, even though Oma hadn't even learned English until high school. Oma went on to run The Bowen Bride, a fabulously succesful bridal gown design shop, until just a few years ago, when arthritis forced her to close the doors and rent out the space.

So even though Oma told some strange tales, Katie'd learned long ago not to question a word. Someone like Oma, whose entire life story paralleled

Bowen's past, spoke the gospel on matters of history, at least in the mind of town residents.

And, as far as Katie was concerned, the expectations resulting from Oma's reputation were the number-one reason to get out of town and go live in a big city. Someplace where you didn't have to speak and act and believe exactly the same as your neighbor or risk being the subject of gossip. Someplace where you weren't subjected to constant retellings of how your grandfather was chosen to lead the Bowen Fourth of July parade back in the Mesozoic era.

Someplace where a girl's main goal in life was something more than simply marrying a good Nebraska man. Yeesh. That was the worst expectation of all.

But until she graduated high school, Katie didn't have much choice in how she lived her life. Thank goodness she'd already been accepted to college in Boston. Only three more months and she'd be free. Of course, she still had to break the news to her father.

She straightened the crocheted armrest covers on her late Opa's wing chair, then plunked next to her grandmother. "All right, Oma. Why's the thread magic?"

The old woman placed the spool in Katie's hands, then wrapped her knotted hands around Katie's. "What most people would find magic is that this thread, it never runs out. When my own Oma, and then my father, told me its secrets, of course I did not believe them. Such a thing cannot be, *ja?* But it is true. My Oma's parents brought this spool with them from the old country. For hundreds of years before they came to America, the family used this thread, but still it is here.''

''Interesting.'' Katie tried to sound as if she believed every word. But wishing to believe for Oma's sake wasn't the same as actually believing. ''So how did this never-ending thread save our family?''

Oma's face crinkled into a smile. ''That is the true magic of the thread. It has the ability to bring lifelong love. Love that lasts through everything, through loss, through pain, even through deception. You might not understand how powerful love can be now, since you are still a child—''

Katie raised an eyebrow, making it clear she did not consider herself a child, but her grandmother merely shook her head.

''What is eighteen when compared to eighty or ninety? You will see. You will experience what the world offers, and you will see that love has incredible power. And this thread, it gives that power. I do not know how it works, exactly, but it does. I used it all the years in my shop, on every single gown I ever made. When stitched into a wedding dress, a couple will stay married forever. I never had a bride who—''

''Katie!'' Katie's dad strode into the room, then shook his head when he spied the thread in his mother's lap. He turned to Katie. ''You're supposed to be straightening up in here.''

"She did. And now I am talking to her," Oma said, defiant. From the expression on her father's face, Katie gathered that he didn't like Oma waxing poetic about a spool of ratty thread.

"If she's done straightening, then she can help me get you ready for your doctor's appointment. You're supposed to be there in twenty minutes."

Oma frowned, but nodded. Katie's dad ducked back out of the room, presumably to find his car keys. Once he left, Oma again squeezed her hands around Katie's. "Take the thread. I want you to have it. And believe in it."

"I'll keep it in my sewing box, all right? Would that make you happy?"

The old woman nodded, then closed her eyes and relaxed back against her pillows. "You will not throw it away? Never?" Her voice came out in a whisper, making Katie wonder if she would fall asleep before her appointment.

"No, Oma. Never." Dad would kill her if she let Oma go to sleep now. "Come on. You need to get up."

"Promise me that you will use it. Just a little will do. In the hem of your wedding dress. Definitely your wedding dress. Promise."

Ha. That's what Oma knew. As if Katie would ever get married. That'd be a one-way ticket to Trapped.

"I promise, Oma. If I ever make a wedding dress, I'll use your thread in the hem."

"Good girl. I'll be watching, just to be sure." Oma

cracked open one eye. "In the meantime, you take good care of your father. He acts as if he needs no one—just the way you act—but I know better. You both need family. Your town, your roots. You will see. And you will teach those values to your own children someday."

Great. More expectations. The meantime was going to be a long time, and her dad definitely didn't want or need to be taken care of. Neither did she. Katie walked to the corner to get the wheelchair. "Let's deal with first things first, Oma."

"First things are unimportant. The thread, Katie, the thread is important."

Katie rolled the wheelchair up to the side of the bed. "Gotcha. Thread is important. Don't trash it. Take care of Dad. Now, let's go."

She threw the thread in her backpack, helped her grandmother into the wheelchair, then let her mind drift to Boston and the adventures that waited there.

Chapter One

The last place Jared Porter wanted to be at 9:00 a.m. on his thirty-sixth birthday was staring through a Main Street shop window at two mannequins wearing wedding gowns. He despised shopping, for one, and for two, flowing yards of silk and lace made his stomach pitch and roll.

Especially when the person needing—no, make that *believing* she needed—the gown was his seventeen-year-old daughter.

How could Mandy do this to him? Or worse, to herself? She was such an intelligent girl, with a promising future all mapped out. In all these years she'd never argued with him—not about anything serious, at least. The fact she picked a fight on this topic… Hadn't she learned anything from his mistakes?

A warm breeze riffled Jared's black T-shirt, lifting

it just far enough above the warm surface of his skin to make him aware of what a scorcher the day promised to be.

Better to get this over with so he could get back to work. He'd already wasted enough time trying to talk himself around it, through it, and out of it. And if he didn't get on-site at the Kleins' new house soon, Stewart would start asking questions Jared didn't want to answer.

And then Stewart—well-meaning, but irritating in the extreme—would assume Jared was having problems at home. And of course he'd want to step in to be sure Mandy was all right. He'd volunteer to help fill out her college applications, go over the quizzes in her SAT prep books—all the academic things he believed Jared didn't understand, though of course he'd never say as much. Things that weren't the problem in the first place.

Jared huffed out a breath, then slid his hand along his waistband to make certain his shirt was tucked into his jeans. Man, he hated working for his younger brother. But he'd brought the situation on himself, and it had taken him this long to position himself to get out. And now he had to figure out how to convince Mandy she could come to regret her teenage choices.

What happened to the days when a parent could lock a seventeen-year-old in her room and simply tell her no? Of course, that's what his parents had wanted to do with him, and the gulf it created between them still existed.

He wasn't about to do the same with Mandy, even if he could.

After taking a quick glance at the store hours posted in the front window, Jared jogged up the three brick steps, then pushed through the glass door, ignoring the overhead clatter of bells that announced customers.

For five minutes, all he needed was his American Express card and a smile, right? He just had to hold it together for five minutes. He could do that—as long as he could keep himself from picturing Mandy standing on the round platform in front of the shop's three-way mirror, giggling about her so-called future with Kevin Durban while some ancient-looking dressmaker crouched beside her, straight pins held in her pinched mouth as she marked a seam.

Or worse, picturing Mandy actually walking down the aisle at Bowen Lutheran.

He turned back toward the front windows and, glancing at his thirteen-year-old blue pickup parked at the curb with its rusted wheel wells and chipped windshield, he wondered if he was doing the right thing. Had all his hard work and sacrifice raising Mandy been for naught? All the careful saving he'd done for her college education a waste?

Don't be like your parents, Porter, he warned himself. *That's the one thing that'll make her go through with it for certain.*

"I'll be out in just a sec," a feminine voice called from the back room. He could hear the rat-a-tat of a sewing machine with its foot pedal pressed, then a rustle of fabric. "That you, Amy?"

"Um, no. Jared Porter."

The sewing machine abruptly cut out. "Oh, sorry. I was expecting Amy Cranders for a fitting."

He turned to see a striking blonde in her late twenties or early thirties emerge from behind the thick blue curtain that functioned as a door to the shops's back room. She raised a can of black cherry diet soda with beads of condensation clinging to the sides. "Can I get you one?"

If the woman was splashed across a billboard holding that can, not a man would continue down the highway without at least tapping the brakes for a second look. Definitely not the elderly woman he'd imagined would run a place like this.

He forced himself to look at the wall clock. "Um, no thanks. If this is a bad time—"

"No, it's fine. Amy's not due for another half hour." She set her drink on the shop's narrow Formica counter, and though her mouth formed a welcoming smile, her hazel eyes betrayed her curiosity. "I've seen you around town a few times, but I'm not sure we've ever formally met." She extended her hand, and he noticed as he took it that she didn't wear nail polish or rings. Probably part and parcel of her profession. "I'm Katie Schmidt. You're Stewart Porter's older brother, right? Stewart was in my high school class.''

''Yeah, I'm Stewart's brother.'' Once again, identified by his younger brother. But when she'd mentioned school, he remembered what Stewart had said about ''that Katie girl.'' Or, more accurately, ''that gorgeous Katie girl.''

Stewart had the gorgeous part right.

''I remember him mentioning you. You're the one who moved to Boston for college, right? Worked in the theater?''

Her freckled cheeks flushed an attractive pink as she let go of his hand. ''For a while.''

He wondered briefly what could make a person who lived in Boston want to return from that life to run a dress shop in rural Nebraska. Especially someone like her, who looked as if she could slide right into city life. He'd never had the urge to leave Bowen, but in his experience those who left didn't come back, no matter what—or who—might be waiting for them back home.

''So what can I do for you, Jared? If you need to rent a tuxedo for an event, I'm afraid I don't handle menswear. I can direct you to a great place in Blair, though. Mention my name and Rosalie will give you a ten percent—''

''I'm actually here for a wedding dress. That is, to pay for one.''

''You are?'' Katie didn't mask her surprise. ''Well,

congratulations, then. I hadn't heard you were engaged.''

No, of course she hadn't, since he wasn't. Despite spending a big chunk of her life living across the country, she would know news like that would be around Bowen inside an hour. When a town's population numbered just under two thousand, everyone knew who the bachelors and bachelorettes were and exactly who was dating whom—or getting married. Women often learned their boyfriends were ring shopping long before the actual proposal came.

"Actually, I'm not. But my daughter is. Well, she might be." He shifted, shoving his hands into his pockets. This wasn't going quite as planned. "If she does, I want to make sure the dress is already paid for so she won't have to worry about it."

"Oh, that's wonderful! Her name's Amanda, right?" Without waiting for confirmation, she explained, "She sometimes baby-sits for my mailman, and he's told me all about her. But are you sure she'd come to The Bowen Bride? There are dozens of shops in Omaha—"

"She'll come here. She keeps busy, and going to Omaha would take up an entire afternoon—or longer. Plus, even if you weren't local, your reputation alone would make her want to come here." He tried not to let sarcasm slip into his tone as he added, "She was very excited by last week's *Gazette*."

Excited being an understatement. The front-page article claimed that no woman who wore a gown from

The Bowen Bride ever divorced, and of course Mandy took that little piece of crazy marketing as a sign. It didn't help that her boyfriend had received a flyer on married student housing with his University of Nebraska application materials the week before— the same day Mandy's best friend, Ashley Harston, announced her engagement, with the full support of the Harston family.

Jared accepted that the Harstons were entitled to make their own choices, and he'd merely raised his eyebrows when Mandy mentioned the housing application over dinner.

But then the newspaper arrived, and Mandy and Kevin suddenly got marriage-happy. As they stood in the living room announcing their plans, he'd remained immobile, sitting on the couch too shocked to speak and unable to believe they were serious. After Kevin left, Mandy went into some convoluted argument about how the article was a third sign, and that threes were lucky. "Kismet," she'd said more than once.

He heard her out, all the time trying to figure out a delicate way to tell her to wait, that urges like this pass when you're seventeen. But she'd slammed out, yelling that he didn't understand.

On the upside, though, her belief in the article meant Mandy wouldn't elope as she'd threatened to in anger. She was too intent on having a dress from The Bowen Bride, and from what he knew, fancy dresses like those Katie made took time.

Katie smiled past Jared, toward a framed copy of

the article, which he now noticed adorned the wall beside the three-way mirror. "Well, thank you. I thought it was a wonderful piece. My grandmother would've loved it. This shop used to be hers."

Ah. So that's how he'd gotten the image of an older woman into his head. Her picture, rather than Katie's, ran beside the article.

She flicked her gaze toward the door, as if a movement caught her notice. As she turned her attention back to Jared, however, she stepped between Jared and the door and leaned her hip against the counter. The subtle change of position was enough to block a passerby from seeing the customers in the shop. Without looking, Jared knew who had to be walking past. Either one of the Montfort sisters, who ran the deli three doors down, or Fred Winston, delivering mail while simultaneously collecting his daily allotment of gossip.

There were days he hated that facet of life in Bowen. Apparently, Katie understood his concern for privacy, which scored her bonus points—though not quite enough to make up for the *Gazette* article. Five bucks said the paper took the content straight out of a press release she'd sent them. It was exactly the kind of thing the *Gazette* did.

He yanked his flattened leather wallet from the back pocket of his Levi's. He needed to fork over his credit card for the dress and get out of there before he became the topic of town gossip. He'd bring the whole thing up with Mandy again tonight, and if he approached it the right way, maybe she'd stop being mad at him long enough to remember she loved him.

Because if she remembered she loved him, maybe she'd realize he loved her, too, and that even though he strongly disagreed with her, he would always do the right thing—like pay for her wedding gown—no matter what the circumstances. He needed to regain her trust long enough to get her to listen to him, slow down for one minute, and decide on her own that marriage at seventeen wasn't a smart move, after all.

"How about this—" Katie pulled out a ledger "—let me get your address and phone number. *If* Mandy does come in, and *if* she decides she'd like me to make her gown, we'll talk about money then. Generally, I take one-third deposit when we agree on the style, a third when we do the first fitting, and the rest when the gown is finished."

"Sounds fine to me." He'd hoped to have the task over and done with as soon as possible, like yanking a splinter from his palm, but apparently that wasn't how one bought a wedding dress. This was going to be more like removing a bunch of splinters—he'd have to go over the area with tweezers several times before all the pieces emerged and the process of healing could begin.

After Katie took down his information, she asked, "So they're still talking about the wedding date? Nothing's set?"

"Nothing firm." At least, he hoped not.

"That's fine. If you can let me know once it's finalized, that'll help with my scheduling. Things can get tight, especially during the summer.'' She looked as if she wanted to say something else, but stopped herself.

Against his better judgment, he leaned forward, putting one hand on the worn countertop. ''What is it?''

He shouldn't ask—it would just mean staying in her shop longer. But now that his task was accomplished and the knot twisting his gut had eased somewhat, he realized that standing in the air-conditioned shop, talking to an incredibly good-looking woman— how had he not noticed her around town before?— might be worth another five-minute delay in arriving at work. Nothing would ever come of it, but every once in a while he craved being able to talk—just talk—to a woman other than his sister-in-law or daughter about nothing in particular.

She hesitated. ''Can I ask something personal?''

''Go ahead,'' he replied, though his brain automatically retorted, *No, Mandy's mother isn't going to be involved in the wedding.* But Katie probably knew that already, or at least knew from the mailman, Mandy's mother wasn't in the picture and hadn't been for years. The dressmaker was going to ask the question anyway, though. People always asked about Mandy's mother. Everyone had loved Corey when she'd lived in Bowen.

''Who's Mandy marrying?''

"Oh." Not the question he was expecting. "Kevin Durban."

Katie's eyes widened in surprise. "Wow. Shows you how fast time flies. I thought Kevin was still in high school. How old is he now? Twenty? Twenty-one?"

"He's seventeen. Mandy, too." Kevin *was* still in high school, for another nine months, anyway.

The knot returned to Jared's gut. He hated thinking about the whole thing, let alone talking about it, but Katie would figure out Mandy's age pretty quickly once the teen sashayed into the shop, fantasizing about marriage despite the backpack full of calculus and AP physics homework slung over her shoulder.

He wanted to stay and chat with Katie about anything other than Mandy and Kevin. But, unsure of how he could turn the conversation to something more interesting—like why Katie had gone to Boston, what she'd thought of life in a busy city, or what had made her return—he thanked her, told her he had to get back to work, then did a quick scoot out the door.

It wasn't until the warm autumn air hit his face that he realized Katie hadn't made any of the comments he'd expected to hear—either the positive comments about young love being a wonderful thing or the not-quite-negative ones about how she was sure Mandy and Kevin loved each other very much.

He wondered if Katie had simply kept her true thoughts to herself or if she planned to discuss them later with her neighbors. Normally he wouldn't care—he'd been the subject of gossip often enough. But he hoped Katie was the type to keep the wedding plans private for Mandy's sake. Mandy might still change her mind about marrying Kevin. But if the whole town already knew about their plans, she might not reconsider. She would get even more caught up in her wedding fantasy, not to mention that her pride might drive her to go through with it just to save face.

And maybe he hoped Katie'd keep mum for his own sake, too. Deep down he wanted to believe a woman like Katie Schmidt could be the upstanding type.

He grabbed the armrest on his pickup and groaned inwardly at the tinny squeak of the hinges as he pulled the door shut. He jammed his key into the ignition and turned it, but kept his foot on the brake, allowing a silver sedan to pull into the spot next to him before he moved the truck. Inside the sedan, he spotted Amy Cranders and her older sister, Joan. Two more single Bowen women now off the market, since Joan had married last month and Amy was now engaged. Not that he'd have dated either of the Cranders, but seeing them pull up to the dress shop made him wonder if life had passed him by.

Raising Mandy on his own meant that dating hadn't been a priority. How bad would things be with Mandy now if he had gone on anything more than a casual date now and then? If he hadn't given Mandy every ounce of his energy once he left work each evening? If he'd allowed himself to just *be* himself, and asked out women like Katie Schmidt whenever the urge struck?

Jared snorted aloud. Since when had he gotten introspective about this stuff?

Probably when he'd flipped over the calendar this morning to see the date.

"You're doing the right thing, birthday boy," he said to himself in an attempt to shake his mood. He backed the pickup out onto Main Street, then shifted into drive and headed to work.

"You finally getting new cabinets and countertops installed, Katie?"

It'd been six hours since Jared Porter's strange visit, but apparently Fred Winston had been thinking about it ever since slowing his walk to stare through her front window.

Not that she *hadn't* been thinking about Jared's visit. It wasn't as if men dropped into her shop regularly asking to buy gowns, let alone a man as handsome and muscular as Jared Porter.

If they had met before, it would have been years ago, and probably only in passing. She'd have remembered the jet-black hair and startling blue eyes, not to mention his height. He had to be at least six-three, and the man was nothing but hard-packed muscle. If she'd known a guy like that in Bowen when she was in school, it might've made her think twice about leaving. As it was, he had her daydreaming at her machine all morning, even though the last thing she needed was a man in her life.

Too many expectations she couldn't possibly live up to.

Unfortunately, Fred's curiosity meant he wasn't going to just drop off her mail and go, leaving her to her work—or to her daydreams.

"What would make you think that, Fred?" Katie eased up on the foot pedal and looked through the open curtain, toward the main room of her shop. For whatever reason, she wanted to make Fred squirm today. He had no reason whatsoever to ask about Jared, other than to gather a little gossip to share at the next stop on his route.

"Saw Jared Porter's truck outside. Since he's the finish carpenter at Porter Construction, and since I'm guessing he isn't fixin' to buy himself a wedding gown, I just put two and two together. You know, he did the chair rail in our dining room last year. All the cabinetry on my neighbor's kitchen remodel, too. Did a fine job."

Katie smiled, glad for Jared's sake that Fred had put two and two together and gotten five. She'd sensed Jared's discomfort from the moment he'd walked into her shop. At first she'd thought his awkward speech and tight expression signaled a simple case of a man ill at ease around such feminine trappings. But when she'd asked about Kevin Durban's age, a switch flipped in her brain and she understood both his discomfort and his unspoken, yet obvious, desire to keep Mandy's plans quiet for as long as possible.

Not that she'd ever gossip about her customers' plans, but in this case, for whatever reason, Katie felt a stronger-than-usual urge to protect a customer's privacy.

"Well, you found me out, Fred. I definitely need a new counter. But I may get a few more estimates before—"

"Nah. Jared's your man. You won't find anyone better—he's a real craftsman. But talk to Jared's brother, Stewart. He's the one who really runs things. He'll cut you a good deal, or at least match whatever other estimates you get."

"Thanks. I'll keep that in mind." *If* she got around to replacing the front counter, which, now that Fred mentioned it, should probably come next on her to-do list of improvements.

And she'd probably just talk to Jared. Stewart wasn't a bad guy, and had a fair amount going for him in the brains department, but *the one who really runs things*? Somehow, after seeing Jared in her shop, she couldn't imagine him playing second fiddle to lean, quiet Stewart. The wide stance of Jared's feet, the way he held his hands on his hips while he was waiting for her to come out of her workroom—none of it pointed to a man who let others push him around. She doubted that very little—with the noticeable exception of buying a wedding gown for his teenage daughter—made him uncomfortable.

Speaking of whom...

"Hey, is that for Montfort's Deli?" Katie nodded to a large package under Fred's arm, trying to keep her gaze—and Fred's—averted from what she saw out on Main Street. "I bet it's the new menus that printer in Lincoln designed for them."

Fred shot her a grin that let her know he'd already scanned the return address. "I hope so. Gloria told me they'd arrive this week. She and Evelyn are dying to see them."

"Well, I won't hold you up, then." After giving him her most friendly smile, she returned to her machine. "I need to get these alterations done by four, anyway. Great talking to you, Fred!"

Fred said his goodbyes, and Katie nearly melted in relief when she heard the bells above her shop door jingle. She waited a few beats, then pushed back from the gown she'd been stitching and strode past the curtain, back into the main room of her shop, to get a better look across the street. Parked at the far curb, Kevin Durban's red Pontiac with the Bowen High School Railroaders bumper sticker was hard to miss. And right there in the front seat, Mandy Porter was kissing Kevin through her giggles.

She had a backpack slung over one shoulder, and it was clear Kevin was dropping her off—she had her seat belt off and the passenger door partially open— but she was having too much fun with Kevin to get out of the car quite yet.

No wonder Jared had looked agitated as he attempted to buy his daughter's gown. This wasn't a couple ready to make a lifelong commitment—not yet, anyway. They were probably as interested in whether or not the Railroaders would win their next football game as they were in marriage.

And thank goodness she'd gotten rid of Fred before he spotted Mandy. Unless Mandy, who Fred claimed was a vegetarian, had developed a sudden desire for a turkey on rye from Montfort's, or her backpack was crammed with laundry for the Suds-o-rama, the young brunette was headed into The Bowen Bride. If Fred saw her in the shop, oohing and ahhing over the gowns, he might add two and two and get four this time.

And since Mandy baby-sat twice a week for Fred's kids, he'd immediately start asking questions. Anything he learned would be carried around town with tomorrow's mail, and Katie suspected that wouldn't sit well with Jared at all. Especially if he wanted Mandy and Kevin to reconsider. Not that Katie wished the youngsters apart, but for a couple their age, she suspected the situation could change in a minute, and they didn't need the whole town speculating about whether their marriage would succeed.

Katie yanked the hair elastic off her wrist, using it to loop her hair into a ponytail. The old air-conditioning unit in her shop would probably work for another summer or two, but she would still get hot if she took Mandy's measurements or rolled out bolts of fabric.

By the time she'd checked her appearance in the mirror in the back of the shop and grabbed another diet soda, the bells on the shop door jangled. Katie strode to the front of the shop to greet Mandy, and when Mandy gave her a timid hello, Katie's insides crumpled.

Chapter Two

Mandy wasn't just seventeen; she was a young seventeen. Fresh-faced and far too unprepared for the ups and downs of marriage.

Until that very moment, when her eyes had connected with Mandy's, Katie hadn't really worried about the idle chitchat about her own shop. She'd let the rumors about charmed wedding gowns and never-ending love persist because, frankly, buzz like that was incredible for business.

Plus, deep in her heart, she liked to think Oma was working a little magic from her perch in heaven every time Katie stitched the hem of a gown using Oma's ratty old thread. If Oma was still alive, she'd have started the rumors herself—and probably would have elaborated on them, telling anyone who would listen that Katie's dresses were even better than those she'd designed and sold for more than thirty years.

But now Katie began to wonder—and to worry—whether the magic might actually be real. Because if it was—if every woman who wore a dress from The Bowen Bride stayed married for life and Oma's thread really did have some kind of magical power—what did that mean for Jared's daughter?

Would she end up happily married to Kevin? Or trapped in a realtionship that wasn't right for her?

What, exactly, did the thread do?

Katie wished she'd asked a few questions—or at least paid more attention—when Oma claimed the thread had mystical properties and tried to explain its importance to her.

"You're Mandy Porter, right?" Katie tried to shake thoughts of Oma as she explained, "Fred Winston talks about you all the time. What can I do for you?"

The teen grinned, happy to be recognized, though the *Kevin + Mandy* scribbled in faded purple marker on her backpack would have identified her to anyone.

"Well, I'm actually here to look at wedding dresses. My boyfriend and I are talking about getting married." Her gaze flitted around the shop, settling on the two mannequins in the window. "Do you have some I could try on?"

"I have several samples in the back, but mostly those are for fit. Everything is custom-made. Do you know what you want, stylewise?"

"Um…" Mandy slowly shook her head.

"That's no problem," Katie reassured her. "I have

photographs of all the gowns I've made in design books, so you can pick and choose which elements you like. You're also welcome to bring me pictures from bridal magazines. We can talk over what you do and don't like and then go from there. All my gowns are one-of-a-kind designs.''

''Oh. So it doesn't work like a regular department store?'' Color crept into Mandy's cheeks, sending a wave of sympathy through Katie. Of course the teen wouldn't know how her wedding dresses were sold—and she shouldn't.

''Not quite. But if your wedding date's close, and you're in a hurry, there are several stores in Omaha that sell off the rack—and they do work just like a department store. There's a lot of variety, and some of the gowns are quite beautiful—''

''No, no.'' Mandy set her backpack on the counter, then turned back to Katie. ''I really want a gown from here. I saw that article on you. You know, in the *Gazette?* When I saw that photograph of your grandmother and read her story, and then that picture of Amy Cranders trying on her dress, it's like, I just *knew*. Kevin thought so, too. Your stuff rocks.''

''Thanks,'' Katie replied, trying not to grin at Mandy's choice of words. ''So, you're not in a big rush, then?''

''No.'' Then the teen put her hand to her stomach, and her already-pink cheeks went as red as the paint on Kevin's Pontiac. ''No! I mean, I'm not in that kind of hurry. I'm not pregnant or anything. We just really love each other and want to get married, you know? We're both planning to go to school in Lincoln next year, and thought it'd be great if we could get a spot in married student housing."

"Of course." She smiled, hoping to put Mandy at ease, though she had to wonder why the high schooler was so fired up to tie the knot. It was something Katie'd always resisted—despite a string of perfectly nice boyfriends during high school and college—which made the fact that she ran a bridal shop a personal joke. But what else was she going to do with her costuming expertise that would enable her to make a living in rural Nebraska?

"Why don't you have a seat over at the table, Mandy. I'll bring out some of the design books. And a drink, if you like."

"That'd be awesome, thanks."

After perusing two books of photos, Mandy glanced up at Katie with a frown. "These are all really pretty. But, um, I guess I should ask—how does the pricing work? I mean, is it less expensive to get short sleeves or a strapless gown? Or a style that doesn't use so much fabric? I'm kind of on a budget."

A tight budget, Katie could almost hear Mandy's thought aloud.

"You don't have to worry about pricing." She tried not to look uncomfortable, but how do you explain to a teenager that her father, who pretty obviously didn't want her to get married, was willing to pay for the dress anyway?

"But—"

"It's been taken care of already." Though, come to think of it, Jared hadn't given her a budget. She'd have to call him to see what he had in mind.

Mandy's mouth dropped open. "Are you serious? Kevin paid for the dress? He came in here already?"

"Yes, I'm serious, but—" As tears of joy welled up in Mandy's eyes, Katie found it tough to continue. "But no, it wasn't Kevin. It was your father. He stopped by earlier today and said he wanted to pay for whatever dress you choose."

"No way," Mandy whispered. "Are you sure it was my dad? Jared Porter? Tall, dark hair, thirty-five years old, good-looking in a dad kind of way?" She hesitated, then covered her mouth with her hand. "Oh, geez. Today's his birthday. He's thirty-six. I'm such an idiot!"

Katie laughed aloud. "You're not an idiot, and, yes, I'm positive it was your father." The man was definitely good-looking, and she wouldn't classify it as good-looking in a dad kind of way. "So don't worry about—"

"I'm not worried about anything."

Mandy stared at the book for another minute, though it was obvious her focus wasn't on the page. Then she glanced at her watch, closed the second book and stood, scooping up her backpack from the counter and looping it over her shoulder.

"I'm so sorry. I totally forgot I'm supposed to be…tutoring a bunch of sophomores in Geometry this afternoon. I'm gonna be late if I don't hustle. But I definitely want a dress. I just—I just need a couple days to think about styles and stuff. I guess I wasn't expecting so many to choose from.''

''That's perfectly fine. Whenever you're ready.''

Katie took a step behind the counter. She'd tried to stay to the far side of the shop while Mandy looked at the books, just to keep the teen from feeling pressured, but apparently she hadn't been far enough.

And she'd obviously said too much. She couldn't remember—had Jared said not to tell Mandy he wanted to pay for her gown? She should have asked him, though this morning she'd doubted the teen would even come in.

Mandy mumbled her thanks, took one of Katie's business cards and shoved it into the back pocket of her faded jeans, then backed out the door as quickly as possible. Katie stacked the design books, but instead of putting them away, she strode to the large windows. Where would Mandy go, since Kevin hadn't waited around?

A minute later, Kevin's Pontiac pulled up to the far curb and Mandy, cell phone in hand, climbed in. She'd gone from confused to agitated, slamming the door as Kevin drove away.

In that moment Katie realized she'd probably set up Jared Porter for an awful evening at home.

Things weren't lining up the way they should.

Jared crouched lower, craning his neck so he could

get a better view of the hinge. He prided himself on getting each and every cabinet door perfectly aligned, every piece of trim straight, every seam invisible. But today the pieces just didn't want to work.

His brain, normally fixed on the task at hand—in this case, the Klein family's new kitchen cabinets—wandered back to Mandy.

And, if he was honest with himself, to Katie Schmidt. Most definitely to Katie Schmidt.

It galled him, because if he was a decent father—and Mandy's actions the past two weeks were starting to make him question that—he'd be solely focused on his daughter and her well-being. Not letting his brain get clogged by a blonde who looked as if she belonged on television commercials offering thirsty men a cold one.

"You nearly done getting those doors on?"

Jared glanced over his shoulder at Stewart, who wore a pristine white polo shirt bearing the Porter Construction logo and a pair of crisp khakis. His cool, unruffled look no doubt meant he'd spent most of his day driving from job site to job site in his air-conditioned minivan while Jared worked in the Klein family's hot, sawdust-filled kitchen.

"Yep. Just need to tighten the hinges so everything's lined up and doing what it's supposed to do."

He wished it was as simple to get Mandy back in line, doing what she was supposed to do. Like focusing on her grades so she'd make honor roll again or studying the materials she brought home from her SAT prep course.

"I need you to stop by the Rivers house on your way home. Janelle Rivers says one of the baseboards in her new addition is cracked, and I'd like you to take a look."

"The guys'll be there tomorrow to install the carpeting?"

"Yep, which is why I'd like you to take a look at it tonight." Stewart leaned against the kitchen island, his gaze sweeping past Jared to study the kitchen's brand-new cherry cabinetry. "Though this is really looking good. The Kleins'll be thrilled when they see it finished, especially with the granite countertops installed and all the appliances in place. The fluted edges were a nice touch."

"Thanks." Stewart had a big heart and meant well, but to Jared the constant compliments still felt belittling, coming from his college-educated, happily married-with-two-kids-and-a-dog, pillar-of-the-community younger brother.

"Since you're headed to the Rivers house, do you want me to pick up Mandy from volleyball?"

Jared twisted the screwdriver with more force than necessary. "They didn't have practice this afternoon, so Kevin was going to take her to the store after school. She said she needed new socks or something... Oh, shoot."

Could he be more obtuse? Volleyball practice canceled mid-week in the fall? And *socks*?

"Jared? Something wrong?"

"Nope." He gave the screwdriver another twist. "Just need to focus on getting this straight."

Could Mandy be out dress shopping so soon? Or worse, were she and Kevin searching around for a reception site? He sucked in a deep breath, then let it out, trying not to take out his anger on the cabinetry. Things were worse with Mandy than he thought. She'd never lied to him before, not since she was four and denied picking all the tomatoes behind their house—while the tomatoes were still green—and trying to feed them to the Eberhardts' cat.

"Okay. I'll leave you to it. But if you or Mandy need anything—"

"Thanks, Stewart. We're good."

Stewart shrugged, then walked out, leaving Jared alone in the nearly completed kitchen. As he finished leveling the final cabinet door, his heart slammed inside his chest.

Why did Mandy feel compelled to lie? And why so dead set on getting married all of a sudden? That was the part he couldn't figure out. She'd never been so stubborn before—they'd always had a high level of trust in their relationship, so even when they disagreed they took the time to hear each other out. The stubbornness had been her mother's defining trait.

He swore under his breath as he stood and used a broad broom to push the sawdust into a pile by the back door. Mandy always believed he'd made a mistake in not marrying her mother, and that had they married that summer they graduated high school—when Cornelia learned she was pregnant—every little thing in Mandy's life would have been perfect. She wouldn't have had to spend her after-school hours shuttling between day-care providers or neighbors' homes, she would have had a mom to volunteer with her Girl Scout troop, she would've had someone to consult about the right style of pants to wear to be the most popular girl in school.

In other words, she'd always wanted a fantasy mom.

But Jared had known, even when he was eighteen and raising hell, that a marriage to Cornelia wouldn't have lasted. Corey very quickly decided she didn't want a baby, didn't want to be in Bowen, and she certainly didn't want a long-term relationship with him. The second Mandy was born, Corey had handed the baby over to Jared, moved to Chicago and never looked back.

Perhaps Mandy thought, in a warped, teenage-logic kind of way, that if she and Kevin got married her whole life would be wonderful. That no one could tell her what to do anymore, that she'd have unconditional love. That Kevin would fill some need for an idyllic family life that Jared apparently hadn't been able to fill.

He cursed again as he leaned the broom against the back door and put away the dustpan.

Well, at least Mandy wasn't pregnant. When she and Kevin announced their plans, she'd stated quickly and emphatically that it wasn't because she was pregnant, and that she had no intention of getting pregnant or starting a family until after college. She insisted she and Kevin both still planned to go to college in Lincoln next year.

Surely she wouldn't lie to him about that—about college or being pregnant. But her attitude toward him the past few weeks bothered him. It had been just the two of them for her entire life, and they'd never had a disagreement like this one.

He wanted her to pursue her dreams in life, but in the right order. College. The astronomy degree she was always talking about. Then a career and marriage, if that's what she wanted. Then, in time, pregnancy and kids.

And he certainly didn't want to envision his daughter having sex prior to marriage anywhere in that lineup. It was the way he'd been raised, and though he never regretted having Mandy in his life, he'd learned the consequences of going against that advice.

When he had recovered from his shock and told Mandy—later, after Kevin went home—that as much as he liked Kevin, and as much as he knew they loved each other, he didn't want her getting married yet, she'd exploded. She'd flashed the newspaper article, then accused him of being cold, of not understanding. After all, how could he, when he hadn't had a serious girlfriend since Corey?

And he'd made the grand mistake of telling her that she should be grateful he hadn't dated anyone seriously since Corey, and that his primary relationship was with her.

Mandy yelled at him to get a life, threatened to elope if he wouldn't support her, then stormed out.

Jared leaned back on his heels to check out the cabinet doors, then rose, strode across the kitchen and checked them again, cocking his head so he'd get a different perspective. Everything lined up, everything as it should be.

In a half hour he'd be at the Rivers house, checking out the baseboard. When he left, everything would be fine there, too. It was what he did. He made things fit. He always took that little bit of extra time to make sure clients were happy, and they trusted him.

Couldn't Mandy trust him the way Porter Construction's clients did? Hadn't she learned in her seventeen years that he would always support her and encourage her and do whatever little bit extra it took to make her happy?

All he could hope for was the dress, and that maybe knowing he'd bought it would wake her up to who and what was important in life. That tradition mattered. That there was a right way and a wrong way to do things, and he wanted her to go about things the right way, as she always had.

He flipped the locks on his toolbox. Then, after ensuring the Klein family's new home was secure, he strode toward his truck, which he'd left parked to one side of the still-unpaved front drive.

If he could get the baseboard at the Rivers house

repaired or replaced in time, maybe he'd swing by
The Bowen Bride again. Though Katie Schmidt said
they could work out the money if and when Mandy
decided on a dress, he hadn't thought to ask the shop
owner to call and let him know if Mandy stopped in.

Would he suddenly get a bill in the mail? How long
did these things take, anyway? He knew clients always needed a timeline for getting their trim work
done so they could plan accordingly. It was probably
no different for Katie creating a wedding gown. De-
pending on the efficiency with which Katie attended
to paperwork, he might get his first bill about the time
the dress was finished.

Mandy and Kevin could be halfway to Las Vegas
with her brand-new gown in the trunk of Kevin's car
before he even had a clue.

As he slid his toolbox to the rear of the truck bed,
he heard the distinctive roll of automobile tires on
hardpacked dirt. Though he didn't recognize the little
blue Volkswagen coming up the drive, there could be
no mistaking the blond driver.

"Hi, Katie." He tried to hide his surprise as she
shut the car door and walked toward him. "Is there
a problem?"

"No, no problem. I was driving by on an errand
and saw your truck." She hooked her thumbs in the
back pockets of her jeans and rocked back on her
heels, suddenly hesitant. "I thought you might want
to know that Mandy stopped in today."

Jared's throat knotted. Partially from Katie's words,

and partially, he was sure, from the way her white blouse opened at the neck, just enough to show off a tasteful expanse of sun-freckled skin.

"She didn't place an order," Katie continued. "Just looked through my design books. But when I saw your truck here, well, I thought you might want to know."

"Yeah. Thanks." He took a few steps toward her, then rested one hip against the wheel well of his truck. "I'm glad you stopped. I was thinking of coming back by the shop tonight."

She didn't say anything, but merely waited for him to continue. There was something tangible skittering in the air between them. Something sending him into the kind of tongue-tied sweat he hadn't experienced since having to get up in front of the class in junior high to recite the Gettysburg Address.

And for reasons he couldn't fathom, she seemed nervous around him, too. Not uncomfortable, not intimidated. Just...aware. As if she sensed the same vibe he did and wasn't sure what to make of it, either.

He cleared his throat, realizing that she was still waiting for him to speak. "Not because I've changed my mind about buying the dress for her. A father should always do that for his daughter, you know?" Jared paused, unsure how much to reveal to her. "It's just—"

"We didn't set a budget." Katie's expression told him what he'd thought—that she hadn't really expected Mandy to come into the shop.

"There's that."

"And she's young."

"Yeah. She's young. And it's not my intention to get you entangled in Mandy's personal affairs, but, well, from a business standpoint, I feel I should tell you that I'm still hopeful she won't go through with it. But I'll pay for your work regardless."

A smile hitched up one corner of Katie's mouth. "I suspected that's how you felt. About Mandy getting married, I mean. I wasn't worried about payment."

Despite the uncomfortable topic, he found himself returning her smile. He bet she did a wonderful job putting her customers at ease, especially since most probably came into her shop stressed out from wedding planning.

"It's just that I want her to be free to do what she wants. If Kevin is what she wants—eventually— that's fine. He's a great kid. But she's always talked about being an astronomer. She gets terrific grades in her math and science courses, and she's taking her SATs next month," he explained. "She's at a point in her life where the options for her future are wide open. I guess you'd understand all that, though."

After all, she'd gone to college out in Boston, and she seemed the self-motivated type, someone who'd studied hard as a teen.

"Well," she said, taking a cautious step forward to lean one denim-clad hip against the hood of his truck, her body just out of arm's reach. "Math and science didn't come naturally to me. I always liked history best. But I understand wanting to pursue your dreams. Everyone can relate to that, I think.''

He wondered if he was crossing the line he'd always tried to set for himself with women, moving from the professional to the personal, but he asked, anyway. "That why you went to Boston?"

A smile played at the corners of her mouth. "I majored in English at Boston University. I told my father I wanted to go into journalism, and even did an internship at a Boston television station one summer."

"You were on Boston television?"

She laughed. "No. I was only behind the scenes. I did get to meet a number of interesting people, though. But my real dream was to do design, so I took a few classes at the New England Institute of Art. It was walking distance from B.U., so it worked out wonderfully for me. After graduation I went into theater work in Boston. Did *Miss Saigon,* a few Shakespeare productions, that kind of thing, designing costumes. It was a lot of fun."

"And now you make wedding gowns."

"And now I make wedding gowns." Her tone remained light, friendly, but anyone with a lick of sense could see from the subtle darkening in her expression that it wasn't a topic she cared to discuss. At least, not the reasons why she did what she did.

Still, he felt she understood where he was coming from with Mandy. After carrying the stress alone for so long, chatting with someone about his daughter—someone who didn't seem to instantly assume he lacked parenting skills—seemed to lighten the load.

"Mandy's lucky you're her father."

Jared glanced sideways at Katie. He could tell, just from the brightness of her hazel eyes, that she meant what she said. It was just what he needed on a day when he doubted himself.

"Thanks." He pushed off of the truck. "And thanks for letting me know she came in today. I wasn't expecting it to be so soon."

"No problem." She took a step back, and at that moment it occurred to him that keeping in touch with the dressmaker over the next few months would mean he'd be able to keep tabs on Mandy and her wedding plans. Plans Mandy might or might not share with him.

"If it's okay with you, Katie, can I ask a favor? Could you let me know what's happening with Mandy? Nothing personal about her relationship with Kevin or anything like that—it's just, well, if she does go through with this, I'd like a heads-up ahead of time. And as awful as it sounds, you might actually know what's going on with her before I do." At least if he and Mandy continued to argue as they had the past two weeks.

Katie's eyebrows shot up. "Jared Porter, are you saying you want me to spy on your daughter?"

Chapter Three

"No. No spying," Jared assured her. "But if you could call and let me know what decision she makes regarding the dress, I would really appreciate it. You know, when she wants it finished or if she tells you a wedding date. I assume she's going to tell me herself, but just in case."

She stared at him for a moment, and he had no doubt she intended to make him squirm. He knew it wasn't her job to report to him, even if he was paying the bills. But still...

He exhaled, knowing he'd asked too much. "I'm sorry. I really shouldn't—"

"I'll tell you what," she said, then jerked a thumb at the tools he'd just stashed in the back of the truck. "You done for the day?"

"Not quite. I have one more quick job. An hour or so, tops. Why?"

"When you're done, why don't you swing by my shop? I need to run a quick errand over in Herman, but then I'll be back in the shop. I think we can work something out. Can you be there by five?"

He nodded, puzzled but curious enough to see what she had in mind. He climbed in his truck and did a quick three-point turn, giving Katie more room to back her own vehicle out without catching a tire in the soft mud on either side of the hard-packed drive. As he passed the Volkswagen, however, he slowed and rolled down his window. She didn't see him at first, since she was turned away to fasten her belt, but when she straightened, she immediately rolled down her window.

"You like turkey?"

When she frowned, he explained. "From Mont-fort's. Mandy's having dinner with one of her girl-friends tonight so they can go over some student council stuff, so I was going there for dinner anyway. I'll bring you a sandwich if you want."

A slow smile spread across her face, instantly warming him. "Turkey would be great. Whole wheat with lettuce and provolone, if you don't mind. And tons of pickles."

Okay, maybe the pickles weren't such a good idea. Maybe none of this was a good idea, starting with her stopping by the Kleins' when she saw Jared's truck in the drive. Because now he was sitting here in her shop, and for some insane reason, she couldn't get her nerves to settle.

Katie pulled her sandwich from the familiar brown paper Montfort's bag, then set out sodas for herself and Jared while he took a large bite of his roast beef on Italian. He sat in the same chair Mandy had occupied only a few hours before, just three feet in front of her at the small table in the shop's main room.

"Evelyn and Gloria Montfort make the best subs anywhere," she commented a moment later, after savoring her first bite of turkey and provolone.

"Mmm-hmm. Mandy's a vegetarian, so she's always giving me looks when I have the roast beef." He took a long drink of his soda, then set it down, staring at the two mannequins in the window for a moment before waiting for her to meet his gaze. "So you said we could work something out. What'd you mean by that?"

So much for small talk. "It's my understanding you build cabinets."

A pair of horizontal lines appeared at the very top of his forehead, just at his hairline. "I do all the finish carpentry for Porter Construction. Trim work. Fireplace mantels. Cabinets when someone wants something custom."

She swallowed a bite of her turkey sandwich. "Well, you need me to do something a little unusual in my line of business and let you know when your daughter comes in. I'm not sure I'm comfortable with that."

"I shouldn't have—"

"Hear me out. I think there's a way for you to keep tabs on Mandy that doesn't require me to call you whenever she comes in. But it'll require you to do something a little unusual in your line of business for me."

She expected him to be wary, but he merely shrugged. "You own your own business. I don't. I work for my brother, Stewart. He owns eighty percent of the company. So my answer is—it depends on how unusual."

She set down her sandwich, then crossed the room to stand behind her battered counter. Using both hands, she gave the entire thing a shove, which caused it to tip about an inch. "As you know, my grandma used to run this shop. I'm afraid this is original. My grandfather installed this for her just before I was born."

"Must be ancient," he teased.

"Makes you wonder how it could possibly be standing," she said with a laugh. "I've been gradually trying to renovate the shop so it looks as nice as the rest of the places on Main Street. Every time I place a bolt of fabric on top of this thing, or someone leans on it hard, I'm afraid it's going to go. But it's been a bit beyond my budget to do anything about it, especially since I did so much exterior work last year, putting in new windows and buying a new awning."

"I see." His eyes twinkled with mischief. "So

you're saying I'm going to have to work for the information?''

"I'd pay you, of course, I just—"

"I'm kidding." He stood, then walked to the counter and placed his hands near hers, giving the entire structure a shake. "If it's just the fact it's loose that bothers you, I could fix that in a jif. And you could always paint the wood to update the look. But I take it you want something entirely new?"

She screwed up her mouth, making it clear she knew he was only being polite. Anyone who wouldn't want a replacement would be sorely lacking in taste. "I loved my grandfather dearly, but truthfully, I feel like it's the kind of thing the Professor might've slapped together for Gilligan and the crew. So yes, a new one is definitely in order, along with a new countertop. I mean, avocado-green Formica? Not even the fact it was installed in the early seventies can justify that. Plus, I want better drawers and cupboards underneath and a shelf at the end, where I can keep my design books. Something more functional, given the way I do business."

Jared took a step back, studied the counter, then walked around it. "You have plenty of floor space. If you wanted, I could even do something a little bigger. It wouldn't impede the walking area, but it'd give you plenty of usable space for office supplies and the shelving you need for your design books. Oak if you want something really durable that looks nice, although distressed pine would look good in here, too.

Pine would hide the wear and tear it'll likely get over the years.''

"I've always liked maple. Light and bright, you know?''

Amusement danced in his eyes. "It's more expensive, but for you, I think I can cut a deal.''

She extended her hand. "That's what I was hoping for. And the same goes for you on the dress. We can work out budgets for both projects that make sense. And I'll cross my fingers right along with you that Mandy opts against marriage. For now, at least. And you'll be able to keep tabs on her yourself, because you'll be coming by the shop to work on the cabinets. I'll just give you a call and let you know when it's convenient for you to come by, if you know what I mean.''

He laughed and took her hand, and she forced down the inward shudder that resulted from his touch. Jared had really nice hands. Strong, capable. "It's a deal. You're going to have the cabinets of your dreams. And thanks, Katie. I really appreciate it.''

She let go of his hand. She shook men's hands all the time. Nothing special about Jared's, right? Just a hand attached to a guy. "Hey, I've been putting off fixing that lousy counter forever, and having you come by the shop gave me the perfect excuse—''

"No, I meant about Mandy. Thanks for understanding. And for not thinking I'm a rotten, evil father, whether you're of the opinion I should just lock her up in her bedroom until she gets over it, or you figure I should butt out and let her run her own life because she's nearly an adult.''

''I'd never think either. She's just at that stage where it's hard to know what to do. Trust me when I say that nearly all girls that age are emotional train wrecks.''

He hmm'd his agreement. ''I just don't want her making a huge mistake.''

Katie returned to her chair, unfolding her Montfort's napkin and flattening it on her lap as she sat down. ''I think any father who encourages his child to pursue her dreams, and who works hard every single day just so she has that chance, is a father who's doing pretty well.''

He shot her a half smile of thanks, then dropped back into his chair and took another sip from his soda. ''Your parents encourage you?''

''It was just me and my dad. My mom passed away very soon after I was born. And yes, he encouraged me—to get married and have kids.''

She couldn't help but grin, envisioning her dad's face when she'd announced that her plans for the future didn't involve staying in Bowen. Or even in Nebraska. ''Not that he wanted me married at seventeen, of course, but let's just say he wasn't especially thrilled when I stood in the living room one afternoon during my senior year and confessed that I'd used some of my spending money to send out a couple extra college applications. I gave him this entire speech I'd practiced about how I wanted to go to school in Boston, since I'd been accepted out there, and about how this didn't change anything between us, and that my decision to move away didn't have anything to do with him. A nightmare of rambling teen logic."

Jared mocked putting a knife to his chest. "Ouch. I feel your father's pain. Though I wish Mandy had only told me she wants to go somewhere else to college. Rebelling by attending a faraway school is one thing. Rebelling by getting married is another. If you decide you made a mistake in your choice of college, you can always transfer. Not so with marriage—at least not without more serious consequences.

A look flashed across his face, and Katie wasn't sure how to interpret it—whether he regretted implying that Katie had been acting rebellious by moving to Boston or whether it was curiosity about why she'd gone—and then come home—in the first place.

The look disappeared quickly, though, and he added, "Don't get me wrong. I like that Mandy's independent. She simply shouldn't take what's best for *me* into her decisions."

"Like deciding to go to a friend's house for dinner instead of celebrating her dad's birthday with him at home?"

Jared froze with his sandwich an inch from his mouth. "Come again?"

"Don't worry—I'm not going to sing. But happy birthday."

He had a smile playing at the edge of his lips as he muttered, "You've got to be kidding."

"I know this isn't the fanciest dinner, but hey, no one deserves to go home to an empty house on their birthday." She did it nearly every year, but then again, she lived alone. Jared didn't.

"Mandy told you?" He said before taking another bite of his sandwich. His demeanor was casual, but she sensed she'd hit upon the truth.

"She did."

The tentative smile broke into a full-fledged laugh. "So you're sure this is all about the cabinets? You didn't just ask me here for a pity date, did you?"

"Well, I guess eating deli sandwiches in a Main Street bridal salon is pretty pitiful, if that's what you mean by a pity date."

"You know what I mean."

She leaned back from the table and studied him. He might be worried and exhausted, between the demands of single parenthood and the time he spent working for Stewart, but he still had laugh lines around his eyes. Definitely laugh lines, not crow's feet. "I legitimately want cabinets. And it can't possibly be a pity date since you're the one who offered to bring sandwiches. And until you offered, I had no idea that you weren't having dinner at home with Mandy."

"Fair enough. I guess I invited myself for a pity date." He polished off his sandwich, then wadded up the wrapper and fired it at the trash can.

"Nice shot."

"Hey, I played varsity for three years at Bowen High. I'd kind of hoped Mandy would play basketball, too. I'm not much good helping her with volleyball." As he said the word *volleyball,* the horizontal worry lines slashed across his forehead again. "So what time did Mandy come in here, anyway?"

"Around three-thirty or so. Not long before I saw you out at the Kleins'." She shot her own sandwich wrapper at the trash can. It skittered around the edge, then fell in. "You think she might've gone home after all? When she told me it was your birthday, she sounded surprised, as if she'd just remembered the date herself."

"Nah. She knows I don't get hung up on stuff like that." He stood, took a final sip of his soda, then carefully set the cup in the trash. Katie had never noticed a male so deliberate with a half-full drink, and she wondered if it came from years of keeping house for himself. He took care not to make unnecessary messes. "Why don't I call you later?"

Katie's stomach did a flip-flop. Was he asking her out? For real, and not a casual get-together, like tonight's?

"Um, sure. That'd be fine." Maybe. A relationship with anyone in Bowen tended to be public, and she definitely didn't want that. Too many expectations, especially when she was just beginning to feel confident and adjusted to her new life and career.

"I'll sketch out a few ideas for your counter and

get you some estimates. Oh, and I'll check my calendar to see when I can get started, assuming you're happy with my ideas.''

Katie nodded as she opened the door for Jared. ''Thanks, that sounds perfect. I'm sure I'll be very happy with anything you do.''

But when he passed her, his black T-shirt brushing her arm, happiness wasn't the first emotion that grabbed her heart. It was more like disappointment. Though why she'd be disappointed Jared didn't plan to call for a date confused her.

She pulled the door shut, then locked it.

Okay, he was a nice guy. He cared a lot about his daughter and her well-being. But Katie wasn't exactly looking for a relationship. At least, nothing more than just a casual partner to accompany her to the town's fireworks display on the Fourth or to sit with at the town's Little League games. Someone who'd bring a six-pack of beer to her house to watch the Super Bowl without making comments about how women didn't get football. Especially since she loved the sport.

Surely she didn't have the hots for Jared, did she? She hadn't really wanted him to say he'd be calling for a date.

No way.

Jared drummed his fingers along the top of his steering wheel as he pulled out onto Main Street. Even though dinner with Katie had been casual, bordering on business related, it left him with the sensation he'd been on a successful, relaxing date. It wasn't a date, of course, even a pity date. But that didn't mean he couldn't mentally pretend for a few days. He needed the break.

Jared punched a button on his dashboard, changing the station from the local sports report. As the trees gracing the rolling hills along the Missouri River started their transition from green to reddish orange, the tension level in the entire state wound tighter and tighter over the latest Cornhusker roster changes. Jared usually got wound up right along with everyone else, but today college talk only reminded him of Mandy and what he could possibly do to ensure she'd be in school next fall—and without already being married.

He needed a rock and roll station, maybe something with a little jump and jive. He surfed stations for a few minutes, then clicked off the radio, deciding that he preferred to let his mind wander back to Katie Schmidt.

Why was she alone? Or was she? Surely there was a significant other somewhere. If there was, Jared envied him. No, he told himself, there couldn't be anyone. Stewart would've said something if ''gorgeous'' Katie was seeing someone. Since he talked to half the town in the course of his business dealings, Stewart was almost as keyed into who was seeing whom as Fred Winston.

Jared reached the end of a bright-green alfalfa field bordering Highway 75, slowed his truck, then turned onto a dirt road that cut a narrow path between the alfalfa and his neighbor's cornfield. A quarter mile later, at a break in the corn, he made a right onto his own long driveway.

He hated coming home to an empty house, but figured he oughta get used to it. No matter what happened with Kevin, a year from now Mandy would be out of the house. Maybe the loneliness just burned a little hotter in his chest tonight since it was his birthday.

He set his mouth as he moved the gearshift into park. Mandy was the best thing that ever happened to him, whether she remembered his birthday or not. He shouldn't be so riled up about it. Kids were kids, and they shouldn't be expected to remember their parents' birthdays.

Though, if she remembered the date and ignored it on purpose...

He stared at his house and cut the truck's engine. He and Stewart built the house with their own two hands. They'd spent nearly eighteen months on it, first in the planning stages, then building the white clapboard house on weekends and during their off hours. In the years that followed, Jared planted trees, adding several to those already standing on the property— strong cottonwoods meant to grant the home some much-needed shade and a natural border to define the neighbors' fields. He'd even built a treehouse in the rear, in one of the older trees, so Mandy would have a place to call her own.

He'd spent the past seventeen years on the sidelines of the dating scene, always wary of letting himself get too close to anyone in particular. At first, because he'd been burned so badly by Corey. But as time wore away at the edges of his pain, and he started going on not only first, but on second and third dates, he still found himself holding back.

After bringing one woman home for dinner, he finally realized why: he'd always wanted Mandy to feel that this was *her* home. It wasn't as if there were dozens of single women in Bowen pounding down his door in an effort to become his wife, given the reputation he'd established for himself back in high school. But even so, he never, ever wanted Mandy to think she played second fiddle to a girlfriend who might or might not become her stepmother. Seeing another woman, no matter how caring or wonderful, standing in his kitchen, opening his cupboards searching for a glass, just felt wrong.

As if he'd betrayed his own daughter, though she'd only been six or seven years old the night he'd cooked his first—and last—dinner at home for a date. The next time he brought a woman home and made her dinner, he had a feeling it'd be because he wanted to marry her.

If anyone could understand the importance and the difficulty of putting off marriage for a more appropriate time, he could. Why couldn't Mandy grasp that?

He spun toward the back seat to reach for his duffel

bag, resolving not to think about Mandy any more tonight. Maybe after he fed the dog he would flip on a late-season Kansas City Royals game and pop himself some popcorn. Declare a moratorium on serious thought for the night, maybe even invite Jim from the lumberyard to come over and have a beer or two and talk about the baseball teams still remaining in the playoffs. Something completely relaxing to celebrate his birthday.

A knock at the window caused him to jump. "Dad?"

"Geez, Mandy."

"You expecting someone else?" She made a show of looking down the driveway for another car as she yanked open his door. "It's about time you got here. I called Uncle Stewart and he said you were fixing a baseboard at the Rivers house. He thought you'd be home by five-thirty, and it's quarter of seven."

"I had another errand on the way." He slung the duffel over his shoulder, then walked to the front door with Mandy at his side. "Besides, I thought you were going to be out tonight."

"On your birthday?" She feigned horror. "As if! Give me a little credit. Maybe I was just getting a surprise ready for you."

"Yeah. *Maybe.*" He shot her a look that made it clear he knew she didn't remember his birthday until late in the day, but Mandy's face split into the grin of a teenager who knew she'd done the right thing just to be there.

"Just come in the house, Dad. You'll see."

"You made a cake, didn't you?" A peace offering. His heart swelled as he looked down at his daughter's sweet face.

"It's in the oven. Should be done pretty soon. And I made you dinner. Spaghetti with lots of veggies."

"You didn't have to do that." He threw an arm around her shoulders and gave her a quick hug before opening the screen door. The aroma of fresh tomato sauce lingered in the air, mixing with the unmistakable scent of a cake baking. As much fun as he'd had with Katie, now he wished he hadn't had that sandwich.

Mandy, about two feet behind him, suddenly stopped short. "Hey. You already ate, didn't you?"

He dropped his duffel and looked around for Scout, their old German shepherd. Probably fast asleep at the foot of his bed, since Mandy would've walked and fed him as soon as she arrived home. "What makes you say that?"

"You didn't run for the kitchen." She held up a hand and ticked off reasons with her fingers. "You didn't tell me you were hungry, and all you said was that I didn't have to do it. You've eaten. And I bet it was something meaty and disgusting."

Couldn't get one past her. "It wasn't disgusting and I wouldn't have eaten, but I thought you weren't going to be—"

"Yeah, yeah. My fault. Just don't mind me while I scarf it all myself." She walked to the stove and prepared a plate. "So where did you eat? Mrs. Rivers have you stay for dinner?"

"No, just in town."

"On your errand?"

"Yep. Hey, you fed Scout, right?"

"'Course I did. He's conked out on the back porch in a food coma. A squirrel went through the yard and he barely even looked up."

She set her plate on the countertop with a clatter. After pulling up a barstool and popping the top on a soda, she stared across the open space toward where he stood in the family room, trying to find the right channel for the Royals game. "So what was the errand?"

When he finally found the game, there was a tarp pulled across the baseball field. Rain delay in Kansas City. "Nothing important."

"Really? Are all your errands not important? 'Cause I happen to know you were in The Bowen Bride today. And that you offered to pay for my wedding dress." A slow smile spread across her face, reaching her eyes and making her cheeks glow pink. "Thanks, Dad. I knew you'd understand."

Jared clicked off the TV, dropped the remote onto the sofa, then strode to the other side of the peninsula counter so he could face his daughter. "Mandy, this is going to come out sounding cold, but...well, I have to ask. Did you come home and make dinner for me because it's my birthday, or because of the dress?"

She wound spaghetti around her fork, but didn't put

it in her mouth. Slowly she set down the fork and crossed her arms. "Both, I suppose. I mean, I would have done it for your birthday alone. And if I didn't, Aunt Vickie and Uncle Stewart would have done—"

"Just so this is crystal clear to you, Amanda, I do not endorse a marriage to Kevin. Or to anyone, for that matter. Not right now. But I didn't want you running off to elope, either. If you're going to do something…"

He reined in his urge to use the word *stupid,* and instead just shook his head, walked around the counter, then pulled up one of the barstools to sit beside her. "Ah, hell, Mandy. I'm just trying to do the right thing, and I don't know what the right thing is beyond telling you not to go through with it. You're practically an adult now, and I want to treat you as such, especially since my parents didn't treat me that way when I decided I wanted to raise you."

"I know, Dad."

"Good. I want you to have a traditional wedding, and I want you to do things the way they should be done. But you're not ready, and I need you to realize that for yourself and wait."

Mandy nodded but said nothing. Jarcd was just about to get up and walk back to the television to see if he could pick up another playoff game—and give Mandy some time to think—when she finally spoke. "Did your errand tonight happen to be at The Bowen Bride, too? Did you have dinner with Katie Schmidt so you could grill her about me? Or did you go somewhere else—like to city hall to check and see if Kevin and I applied for a marriage license?''

Jared let out an exasperated breath. ''Of course I didn't go to city hall. But if you must know, I did have dinner at the dress shop with Katie. She saw my truck at the Kleins' and stopped. She wanted me to look at her counter, since it needs to be replaced. Since I thought you were going to be out tonight, I decided to grab a sub from Montfort's with her.''

Mandy's face went red. ''So you're not having her spy on me or anything?''

''No.'' A lump of guilt rose in Jared's chest and he forced himself to ignore it. ''But I'm designing new counters for her, so I will be around her shop.''

Silent, Mandy picked up her fork again, apparently absorbing what that would mean for her. He clicked on the game—the Royals were out on the field now, though rain still threatened—and pushed off the barstool to scoop some spaghetti onto a plate despite already having eaten. Though he sat beside her, Mandy hardly looked at him. Instead, she stared at the television, not even cheering when one of the Royals knocked a ball out of the park. At a commercial break between innings, he loaded their dishes into the sink while she wordlessly frosted the cake.

Some party, he thought.

When he closed the dishwasher, she set down her spatula and looked at him. ''Did you have a date with Katie, Dad? An actual *date?*''

''Honey, I just met the woman today. We were

talking counters and eating sub sandwiches. No candles, no romantic dinners, so don't even think it.''

''Oh.'' She handed him the spatula so he could lick off the frosting, just as he had for her when she was little. She watched him carefully as she spoke. ''But I do think it'd be really good for you. To date, I mean.''

Chapter Four

Jared stopped working on the spatula and stared at Mandy. "You want me to go out on a date? With Katie Schmidt, the dressmaker?"

"Well, with *somebody*, though I think Katie'd be an awesome choice. I assume you know what to do. Or at least you did once, since I'm here."

"Hey, now—"

"So, what do you think about her, Dad?" Jared couldn't help but wonder at the sudden sparkle in Mandy's eyes. "She's cute, isn't she? And there's just something about her that's, like, magical. I could totally be a matchmaker for you. Totally. She'd go out with you. You're decent looking and nice and all. If you weren't my dad and old as dirt, I'd consider you hot."

He rolled his eyes as he dropped the spatula into

'the appropriate slot in the dishwasher. ''Mandy, she's not magical, no matter what they wrote in the *Gazette* article. And I definitely don't need you playing Cupid for me. You've got enough going on as it is. If I want to date, I'll date.''

But even as he said it, he knew it wasn't true—either the part about Katie not being magical or the indifference he feigned. Something intangible and in-explicable about Katie—something beyond her warm smile or her ability to understand his situation—called out to him, made him want to spend time with her and learn more about her.

''You liked her, huh?'' Mandy's voice was low and serious, as if she'd just read his thoughts.

''Is this sudden interest in my love life meant to distract me from yours?''

''Maybe. Thing is, no matter what's going on with me, you really should get out there, Dad. I'm an adult now, or almost—you said it yourself. You don't have to worry about bringing some woman home and hav-ing her tell me what to do, because I'm old enough now to tell her to take a hike.''

''I never—''

She waved off his argument. ''And you're not that old. I mean, you're about the same age as Ben Af-fleck, and look at him. You should be out there dating and hooking up with women.''

''Please don't compare my life to Ben Affleck's.''

''I'm just saying—''

''I know what you're saying. Don't.'' He grabbed

a knife from the drawer and pointed it. "Pass me that cake. Let's skip the candles and just eat."

She laughed and slid the pan across the countertop, then opened one of the pine cupboards to hand him a plate. "Well, if you know what I'm saying, promise me you'll think about it."

"Mmm. Great cake, you should have some." He grinned as he picked a crumb off the edge of his plate, making it clear that Mandy should drop the subject.

But as he strode to the couch with his plate, he couldn't help but think.

What would Katie say if he did ask her out?

After the cabinets went in, Katie figured she'd need to put aside funds to have the air-conditioning overhauled earlier than she'd planned. Winter might be coming in a few short months, but she'd been dying all afternoon.

Well, at least since Jared arrived.

After using the back of her arm to swipe a few beads of perspiration from her forehead, she rose from her sewing machine to wash her hands. Didn't want to risk sweating all over Amy Cranders's gown. Tomorrow it would be done, and after Amy came in for her final fitting, it'd be time to stitch Oma's thread into the hem.

As she turned off the warm water, she let her gaze drift across her workroom to the large pegboard where she stored her oversized spools of thread. Oma's thread rested at one end, on the highest peg.

How many gowns had their hems stitched with that thread? There had to be a way to find out, though she suspected Oma hadn't been much for keeping records. And even if she had, those records probably weren't in the shop—everything had been cleared out after Oma's death, while her father rented out the shop to a stationer.

She glanced through the drawn-back curtain toward the front room—and the reason for the added heat in the shop. Jared crouched near the floor, his back to her, and cocked his head to look down at the yellow measuring tape he'd extended across the front of her old counter. He spun on the toes of his work boots, scribbled something on the wire-bound notebook on the floor beside him, then slid the tape along the other side of the counter.

Katie was just about to sit back down at her machine when he caught her staring.

"Hey, Katie. If you've got a minute, I have a couple ideas I'd like to show you."

"Um, sure." She wiped her palms on her jeans, then strode out to the front.

He set his notebook on the counter, flipping to a page further back. "I came up with three different ideas. One would have the cabinets in the same footprint they occupy now, two would be slightly larger. The larger ones would give you an extra shelf on the end, which could hold up to twelve design books, assuming you stick with the same size books. I think it's worth taking up the extra floor space. You still have plenty of room.''

"Wow.'' She looked down at his detailed drawings. He'd listened closely to every word she'd said the previous night, because he'd managed to incorporate every amenity she could want into the design. Not to mention that he'd taken the extra time to measure her design books to be certain they'd fit the space.

"Would any of these work for you?"

"Are you kidding? I'd be ecstatic to have any of them.'' She flipped a page to look at one of the other designs. When he pointed out some of the shelves, she shook her head. "I don't know that I'd ever have that many books—a customer wouldn't want to go through that many, even if I offered that many options. But I love the look of this design. Graceful but functional.''

"I could put doors on this lower shelf.'' He spun the sketch so she could better see what he meant. "Built that way, you could put design books there if you wanted, or use it for whatever. There are three drawers here, and plenty of structural support so you could put whatever you wanted on the countertop. It'll be a real workhorse.''

Their fingers bumped when they both went to flip to the pervious page, and Katie fought the urge not to yank her hand back. "It's all fabulous. When did you draw these?"

"Just now. I had to double-check the measurements."

She swallowed hard, trying to get control of herself. What was it about Jared? Had she been sequestered away from men—well, other than Fred Winston or the occasional groom-to-be who got dragged along to the shop to help pick a gown, in spite of tradition—for so long that she couldn't be casual around them anymore? She'd dated plenty of guys in Boston, and Jared wasn't like any of them.

But maybe that was just it. He wasn't like any of them. He was a typical Nebraska man, and you didn't find many of those in Boston. Maybe she'd been stupid to have such a knee-jerk reaction to local guys just because that was who her family expected her to date.

"Is something off, Katie? I'm happy to adjust—"

"No, no." She shook her head. "I really like them. But will these fit in my budget?"

He grinned. "Definitely, including the countertops, though Stewart would order those from another subcontractor, a company we use out of Blair. I thought you could do Formica again—since it's reasonably priced and much better looking these days than what you currently have. Maybe with a beveled edge to match the wood on the cabinets."

He'd thought of absolutely everything. "That sounds perfect. And all this is okay with your brother?"

Jared nodded, but his dark eyes flickered, and Katie

knew she'd said the wrong thing, making it sound as if she assumed Stewart had to approve anything Jared did. And while he probably did, she shouldn't have reminded Jared of that fact.

"I know you're giving me a great discount. I really appreciate it and all the time you put in on this. I'm impressed."

"It's nothing." A smile played in his eyes, and Katie's heart did a slow flip inside her chest. "I usually work on bigger projects—doing all the trim and cabinets in a brand-new house—so a small project like this is fun for me. Gives me a bit of a break. Plus I almost never get to work in town. I don't have to bag my lunch for once."

"It's a lot healthier to bag it. I always grab my lunch from upstairs, since I live above the shop, though it's tempting to toss my salad in the trash when practically everyone who walks by my store window between the hours of eleven and two is carrying something from Montfort's."

He shook his head. "You seem like the type who could eat all the Montfort's you want—with all the fixings."

"I'll take that as a compliment. Though the place I really want to try is Celestino's, that new pizzeria over in Herman. Been there?"

"Nope, but Mandy has. She really liked it—said it's run by a young Italian couple who moved up from Omaha. Apparently they're very friendly and have adjusted well to life in Herman. Even started going to the biweekly bingo games. I've been wanting to go there for a while, myself. Celestino's, that is. Not bingo.''

He swiveled the notebook so he had the drawings facing him again. He tapped his pen against it and opened his mouth to say something, then stopped short.

Katie frowned. ''What?''

''So let's go.''

Did he just ask her out? ''To bingo? Or Celestino's?''

''Celestino's. You busy on Friday?''

She tried not to grin at the way he suddenly stopped tapping his pen, or at the faint blush tingeing his cheeks. She suspected it had nothing to do with crouching on the floor to double-check his measurements. Jared Porter, a super-buff, super-masculine, I-own-every-tool-known-to-man type, had a wicked case of nerves.

''You're asking me for a date?''

''Uh, yeah. I guess I am.''

At his embarrassed smile, she wanted to melt. Jared Porter was the perfect man for her—on paper, at least. Nonjudgmental, unlike Brett, the last guy she'd dated in Boston. Plus he was a hard worker, creative, funny and definitely easy on the eyes. The man had a firm, full mouth that screamed to be kissed.

She really wanted to go. She wanted to see if Jared could relax and have fun, if he could forget for an hour or two that he had a teenage daughter. She wanted to see if he put red pepper flakes on his pizza or if he was a parmesan cheese kind of guy.

The idea of spending an evening letting herself kick back at Celestino's, laughing about town events and not worrying about whether or not she'd exercised bad judgment simply by saying yes to a date seemed realistic with Jared. She could even picture him pulling his truck into the parking lot, then walking around to open the door for her, just because it was the sort of thing she suspected he'd do.

That was the frightening part. It was all too easy to imagine.

She looked down at his fingers where they rested near the edge of the notebook and imagined his hand moving over the page, sketching out the various options for her cabinets, his brow furrowing as he thought through each stroke of his pencil, assessing what features would be the best.

She'd do the same for Mandy—assuming Mandy and Kevin went forward with their plans to marry— settling down to assemble all the components of a perfect wedding gown. But if what her grandmother told her about the thread was true, then what? Should she stitch in that final, enchanted length of thread?

Or was she being silly to even think about it? The thread couldn't really have any special power, could it?

"I'm sorry, Jared, but I probably shouldn't." She felt her color rising as she added, "And not because of you—I mean that. It's just…there are just other things—''

''No explanation necessary.'' He shot her an amused look. ''But, hey, you can't blame a guy for asking. It might be awkward, anyway, with me working on your cabinets. I want you to be able to tell me straight out what you do and don't want without thinking, 'Gee, I can't tell him I don't like that beveled edge, especially after he spilled his soda all over me at dinner and felt so bad about it. I might hurt his feelings.'''

Katie couldn't help but laugh in response. ''I'd never hold a soda spill against a guy.''

He tore the pages out of the notebook, then passed them to her. ''Look these over and take a day or two to think about what you want. Then give me a call.''

''Sure. And thank you.'' She already knew what she wanted. She wanted to give him a call despite the fact he hadn't even left the shop, but the call had nothing to do with cabinets.

As the glass door shut behind him, leaving behind only the echoing jingle of bells, and he gave her one last wave as he backed his pickup out of one of the diagonal spaces that fronted her shop, Katie wondered if she'd ever be able to trust in herself enough to date a man again.

He'd been completely, one hundred percent insane to ask her. He should've known it'd go badly when he decided to accept dating advice from his own daughter. What thirty-six-year-old in his right mind did that?

But even though he'd been turned down flat, he didn't regret it. She'd wanted to say yes. He wasn't an expert on women, not by a long shot, but he knew it with every fiber of his being.

If Katie'd been a curiosity to him before, now she'd become a mystery he wanted to solve—even though common sense said to leave it alone. One week after he'd last walked into her shop, he still couldn't get the gorgeous blond dressmaker out of his head.

Jared unloaded his toolbox from the back of his truck, watching as Katie stood in the next parking space, helping Amy Cranders lay out her new garment bag-encased wedding gown across the back seat of her silver sedan.

Once Amy pulled away, Katie turned to Jared and rested her hands on her denim-clad hips. "Great timing. Unless I have a drop-in, the store will be empty the rest of the afternoon."

Leaving the two of them alone, in other words. Jared secured the truck's tailgate, then gestured for Katie to lead the way back into the shop. "How about tomorrow?"

"No appointments scheduled. You can hammer and saw to your heart's content." She opened the door wide so he could carry in his tools—and stood back just far enough to keep him from accidentally brushing against her. "And you think this'll only take a couple days? That's hard to believe."

"I'll take out the old counter this morning, then I'll need to go back to my place to get the components for the new unit. Stewart will help me load it up and deliver it here. Tomorrow I'll install it and put on the doors. The trim will be the day after that—I'm almost finished with it—and the countertop will be last. He's hoping to be here Friday or Saturday, if that works for you. Probably Friday."

"Can't wait."

They were dancing, he could tell. Each of them testing out the other to check their comfort levels. And no wonder. You generally didn't ask a woman out, get turned down, then only a week later come into her shop and proceed to spend several days alone with her, especially when you were both adult enough to understand that an attraction existed.

"So you do a lot of your woodworking in your house?"

"My basement is one big wood shop. Plenty of room for my equipment and whatever pieces I'm working on, so I don't need to be on job sites all the time. It's perfect when I need to be home for Mandy. I love working down there, but Mandy calls it my hole," he laughed. "She doesn't go down there unless she has to."

"I can relate." Katie pulled the glass door shut, then watched him as he unloaded his tools and cleared space around the old cabinet so he'd have room to work. "My Oma—my grandmother—used to run this shop. When I was a kid I visited all the time, but I never wanted to go into her workroom in the back. I called it The Pit. It was perfectly clean and organized, but it was her space. I felt like I was intruding. Now I love it. Even though I live upstairs, I come down here at all hours to work. It's relaxing to me."

"Somehow I don't picture Mandy or her children taking over my basement workroom," he replied, though even as he said it, it made him wonder how far off grandchildren would be. At thirty-six, he wasn't anywhere near ready to be a grandfather. Then again, he hadn't been anywhere near ready to be a father at eighteen.

"You never know, though," Katie argued. "I had to go away for a while, first. If you'd asked me when I was a teenager whether I wanted to run The Bowen Bride, I'd have laughed in your face."

Jared set his crowbar on the Formica countertop. "Going away made you appreciate it?"

"Believe it or not. And Mandy will appreciate what you do, too. Though you're right—I can't picture her wanting to spend an afternoon sanding or finishing someone's built-in cabinetry." One side of Katie's mouth curved up. "But when she's older, she'll go to the basement and picture you there, working. It'll be a great memory for her. Bet she even tells her children about it."

Jared nodded, unsure he wanted to discuss Mandy—or the possibility of Mandy being a mother someday—with Katie, but he still found himself reassured by her words.

"No matter what she does now, she'll find her way home, Jared. She's just that type."

"You sound like you're speaking from experience."

"I am." This time it was Katie who seemed unsure she wanted to continue the conversation. She stepped toward the windows, where the two mannequins stood. "I assume you're going to be kicking up a lot of dust. If you could help me move these to the back, I'd appreciate it."

"No problem." He lifted one of the gowned mannequins from the raised area by the window, then carefully walked it to the back, so he wouldn't accidentally step on the long train with his work boots. He ducked through the curtain, looked around until he spied an empty corner of the workroom off to his right, then set the mannequin down. "This all right?"

"Perfect," Katie said as she entered behind him and set the second mannequin beside the first.

"There shouldn't be too much dust today," Jared explained. "Or tomorrow, when I'm installing the main unit. But there will be when I finish the trim. I'll sweep after I'm done, but you might want to keep the workroom curtain drawn, just to protect all this fabric."

"There's actually a sliding door I can use to close off this area," she said, pointing. "I hardly ever use it, but if the dust gets really bad, I'll just pull back the curtain and close the door."

He looked around at the large bolts of fabric, each

on its own giant spindle. Most were in different shades of white, but there were a few in pastel and jewel tones, presumably for bridesmaids' dresses. Beyond that, a large black file cabinet stood next to a set of shelves holding what appeared to be financial books. A large worktable and two sewing machines stood in the center of the room, and a large pegboard with row upon row of thread dominated the far wall. Everything was neat and organized, just as he'd suspected. The room reflected Katie perfectly. Anyone could walk in here and find whatever they needed in an instant. No bride who saw this room would have a second thought about a gown being delayed or worry that she'd get anything other than exactly what she wanted. No one this organized failed to keep her promises.

"You've made this area very professional," Jared commented. "Much nicer than I imagine most workrooms are. It's obvious you enjoy running your own shop."

"I do." She bent to adjust the train on one of the mannequins' gowns so it was out of the way. Without looking up, she asked, "How about you? You enjoy working with your brother?"

He wondered if that was part of what stopped her from accepting his invitation to dinner. Did she view him as a working-class guy, someone without the same level of education she'd obtained, and therefore maybe not the best person for her to date? As someone less sophisticated and rough around the edges?

Corey had certainly seen him that way.

"Stewart's great." Though if things went well, he might not be working for Stewart much longer. He'd saved up almost enough to open his own shop, doing what he really loved—refinishing and repairing furniture—a real feat, considering he'd also been saving up money to send Mandy to college ever since she was born. He just had to go about it in such a way as to make sure Stewart wasn't stuck without a good finish carpenter.

He wondered if knowing his future plans would have made a difference in Katie's response to his dinner invitation. If it did, he didn't want to know. Being picky was fine and dandy, but being picky without reason wasn't. Shades of Corey he never wanted to see in another woman, even if Corey'd only been a confused teenager at the time.

He was just about to walk back to the front room when an out-of-place object caught his eye. Without thinking, he strode to the opposite side of the workroom for a better look.

"Was this thread your grandmother's?"

Katie started to answer, then hesitated. "What makes you think that?"

"It's older. Lots older. Rougher texture." He couldn't help but grin as he looked at her over his shoulder. "I'm a detail person. Didn't mean to ask anything intrusive."

It was probably intrusive enough just to be standing in her workroom. Not only had she said it was her special space, but from where they were standing in relation to the curtain, no one could see them back here. If someone walked in the front door and the two of them walked out, they'd wonder.

"It's not intrusive. You're just observant." Katie came to stand beside him. "And you're right, it was my grandmother's."

"Something sentimental, then?"

"I suppose." She was only inches off his elbow in the narrow space between the worktable and the pegboard. If he wanted to, he could wrap an arm around her, as he so often did to Mandy. Tuck the stray hair back behind her ear or kiss the top of her head.

But it would be nothing like with his daughter. That was comforting, the act of a loving father. Katie stirred entirely different emotions. Emotions that would have him kissing a lot more than the top of her head.

"We're a lot alike, I think," Katie said, looking at him sideways. Her hazel eyes had a glint in the corners, reflecting the light streaming in from the front room.

"I never went to college, like you did. Never lived anywhere but Bowen," he commented. "And I doubt you have a teenage child sitting in study hall over at Bowen High."

"No, but that's not what I meant. That's all cosmetic."

He turned slightly, just enough to meet her gaze. They were treading dangerous ground now, and he wasn't sure it was his place to push ahead. She'd been the one to turn him down, not the other way around.

"Not as much as you might think."

"I disagree." Her gaze fell on the old spool of thread, then back again. "And I've been thinking, maybe I was wrong."

What did that mean? "About us being alike?"

"No. Last week."

He suddenly grasped that she meant about Celestino's, but he had to hear it from her.

If she said it, though, then what? His stomach clenched as a slow blush crept along her high cheekbones and she exhaled. Was he ready for this? After all the years of failed half-relationships, of focusing on his daughter first and himself second, was this the right person and the right time?

Because more than anything, he wanted to kiss Katie Schmidt. To hell with cabinets and wedding gowns and what Mandy might or might not think.

"What were you wrong about last week?" he asked, his throat constricting against his will, even as the question left his lips.

She tipped her head, then tucked a loose blond strand behind one ear. "I think I was wrong about Celestino's."

Chapter Five

"I should have said yes."

Katie held her breath, partially because she couldn't believe she'd admitted it aloud, partially out of embarrassment at reversing herself.

And partially because she thought Jared just might kiss her.

Despite the mixture of fear and desire coursing through her at the sight of him standing not two feet away from her in a clean white T-shirt, with his work-hardened hands resting casually at his waist, and despite common sense telling her that, given the bad judgment she'd exercised in the past, she was better off not getting involved with anyone—let alone someone like Jared, who probably had a busload of baggage and needed to find a woman more perfect than she could ever be—she wanted him to kiss her.

Who in their right mind could resist someone as dark and handsome as Jared? A man who not only loved his family, but who had a chest perfect for leaning into and smiling against, with powerful arms capable of making even her feel secure?

She exhaled at the thought of her fingers spread out across his shoulders, pulling him closer. Every instinct told her that kissing Jared would blow her mind, and if she took that chance right now, she'd gladly live with the ramifications.

He took a step forward at the exact same moment the bells on the shop door clanked against the glass and footsteps sounded on the hardwood floor.

"Hi, Katie! You stitching your fingers off back there?"

"Fred Winston?" Jared whispered, amusement lighting his clear blue eyes. "And you thought I had great timing when I showed up."

"Classic Fred," she hissed back, half disappointed and half relieved. She called toward the front of the store, "I'll be right out."

Jared winked at her, which made her grin in response. Out loud, he added, "That you, Fred?"

Fred's footsteps ceased. "Jared? Jared Porter?"

"Yep." Then, in a whisper to Katie, Jared said, "As if he didn't already see my toolbox."

Katie looked down at her sandals so Jared couldn't see how hard she was trying not to laugh. "Jared's helping me move the mannequins," she managed.

"Celestino's?" he asked, his voice barely audible.

"Surely I can entice you with a large pizza, extra cheese?"

"How about Friday?"

He gave a slight nod, then spun away from her and walked out to the main room, leaving her to follow behind.

"How're you doing, Fred?" Jared made a show of brushing his hands against his jeans, as if he'd been carrying a load of lumber into the workroom instead of a mannequin in an alabaster wedding gown.

"Fine, fine." The mail carrier made no attempt to hide his curiosity, but as he withdrew Katie's mail from his shoulder bag, he noticed the crowbar on the counter. He blinked, then looked again to Jared, who'd already turned away to grab a mallet from his toolbox.

"Katie mentioned that she was fixin' to get her cabinets and countertop replaced." Instead of dropping the mail on the-counter, as he usually did, he held it out to Katie. "Glad she had the good sense to hire you. I told her to call Stewart and set it up— you're the best around."

"I appreciate the referral, Fred."

Katie interrupted as she accepted her stack of mail. "Actually, I never did talk to Stewart. But I do agree with you, Fred. Jared's the best around."

A light furrow crossed Fred's brow, so Katie reached over to her table, moving a design book so she could show the mailman Jared's sketch. "This is what Jared's building for me. He had three different ideas sketched out, with the shelves and drawers in different configurations, but I like this one best. What do you think?''

''Mighty nice,'' Fred agreed, distracted from whatever he was going to say. ''Well, I'd best get going. I'm behind on the route today. Can't wait to see the finished product, though.'' He nodded a goodbye to Jared, shifted his mailbag a little higher on his shoulder, then strode out.

Katie glanced at Jared, wondering if his mind was still on what was happening before Fred interrupted. However, he already had one hand on the top of the counter while he used the other to push against the side so it tilted slightly, lifting off the floor.

''Good thing this is already loose,'' he commented. ''Should make it easier to remove. I'll be careful not to scratch your hardwood floor.''

''Thanks.'' As charged as their conversation was before, Jared seemed awfully businesslike now. She wondered at the change—this was more than a simple interruption.

And as she watched him test the edges of the counter, she thought she understood.

He angled his head toward the table. ''Might want to put your design books in the back, just in case. I'll move the table if it gets in the way.''

''Fred doesn't mean to be a jerk,'' she said.

''He wasn't.''

''About Stewart. I mean, he didn't need to make that comment.'' Just as she shouldn't have asked

Jared last week if he'd checked with Stewart to be certain the estimate he'd offered was okay.

Jared shrugged. "Hey, Stewart's the boss. Nothing wrong with that."

But despite Jared's nonchalant air, she got the feeling there *was* something wrong with it—in Jared's mind, at least. She tried to think of an appropriate response, but as Jared wedged his crowbar under one end of the old cabinet, he added, "You don't have to defend me."

"I wasn't."

He glanced at her and raised an eyebrow.

"Okay, so I was. But that wasn't my intention. I just thought Fred was being rude and I didn't like it. It's not as if I look at him and say, 'Hey, don't you need the permission of the postmaster general before you rummage through my mail and comment on it?'

That drew a smile out of Jared. "People think what people want to think, Katie. Folks around town thought it was wonderful when Stewart went through Bowen High a couple years after me, got all As and went on to Lincoln with a scholarship to cover half his costs. Whereas I'd been nothing more than the B-level screw-up who got the homecoming queen pregnant and then didn't even have the decency to marry her. Working for Stewart and crafting a quality product is a huge step up for me in the minds of most people. Doesn't bother me. They're entitled to their views. That's just how small-town life works. There are upsides, too."

Didn't she know it. Though, how Jared took it so easily was beyond her, when she'd struggled with living up to small-town expectations all her life. He had an ability to blow off the opinions of others she didn't have.

"So what's the truth?" she asked.

He shrugged as he lifted the crowbar, moved it a few inches along the underside of the cabinets, then lifted again, his biceps bunching as he separated another section of the old cabinet from the floor. "I'd rather be my own boss, but if I'm going to work for anyone, Stewart's the best. He really is a good guy."

"And so are you. You're no—" what had he said? "—B-level screw-up."

"You know that for a fact, huh?"

"It's a gut instinct. And I'm entitled to my opinion, too." Though her instincts hadn't been accurate when it came to guys in the past. That was part of the reason she'd come back to Bowen, where she felt surprisingly centered. But there was an honesty about Jared that even his flippant tone couldn't hide. He might've been wild in high school, but he wouldn't have treated anyone badly, especially not a girl pregnant with his child. He wouldn't have abandoned her, just as he hadn't abandoned Mandy. Something had happened there that the townspeople didn't know about, and Jared was keeping it to himself.

She pulled the small table closer to the back of the shop to give Jared room to maneuver around the counter, then gathered up her design books.

Before ducking through the curtain, she asked, "So have you ever thought of opening up a shop for yourself? Or would that present a problem—competing with your own brother?"

"I'd never do anything that would directly compete."

So he *had* thought about it. She wondered how detailed his plans were. "Well, for what it's worth, I think you'd do just fine running your own business. Everyone in town knows your work and your reputation. And if they don't, Fred's willing to tell them."

A low chuckle escaped him as he moved the crowbar, then used the mallet to loosen a section. "That's what I'm afraid of."

"Jared—"

He paused in his work, and his blue eyes found and held hers. "Celestino's."

The look—and the single word—sent a wave of anticipation through her. "Friday."

She ducked back through the curtain, unwilling to let him see how he rattled her. As she set her design books on a clear section of the worktable and grabbed her appointment calendar to see whose gown she needed to work on next, she tried to ignore the thumping in her chest.

What had she gotten herself into?

When Jared pushed through the door to Katie's shop the next morning, he heard the pedal on the sewing machine pause, then resume, the pat-a-pat going slightly faster than before.

He'd made her nervous.

"Morning, Katie," he called out, then added, "It's just Jared." Though she'd probably already made that assumption.

"Good morning. I'm midseam right now, so excuse me if I don't come out. Help yourself to a soda if you want one."

Polite, friendly, but keeping her distance for the moment. Probably the right move, he mused, while he lifted the now-disassembled sections of Katie's old cabinets from where he'd stacked them the previous day and carried them one by one out to his truck. The woman was far too perceptive, and he'd already said more to her than he should have, both about what happened—or hadn't happened—with Corey and about his plans for someday leaving Porter Construction.

For the rest of the morning, they each worked on their own side of the half-open curtain, keeping to themselves. He made a trip back to his home workshop, where he met up with Stewart, and together they loaded up the base sections of Katie's new cabinets and took them to the bridal shop. Stewart made small talk with Katie whenever Jared ran out to the truck, but Katie retreated to the back while Stewart helped Jared line up the heaviest sections.

"I think I'm good to go now," Jared told his

brother as he finished adjusting the largest section. "I can handle the rest on my own."

"I'll head over to the Rivers house, then. See if they'll be ready for you to install the shelves in their new addition when you're done with this project." He said his goodbyes to Katie, then headed out.

When the door jingled closed behind him, Katie stepped out into the main room.

Jared tilted his head in the direction Stewart had just gone. "Told you he was a good guy."

"Never said he wasn't."

Jared turned back to the new cabinets, his nerve endings instantly electrified. When he'd asked her for the date, he hadn't considered how awkward it'd be to work in her shop in the days leading up to the event. Having her turn him down—then go on to accept the date—just made things more complicated.

Not to mention the fact he'd come darned close to kissing her yesterday, and she'd known it. She'd leaned in closer, held her breath, bit her lip.... No guy could miss the signs. And he was certain he'd been giving off signs of his own. Couldn't help it, really. Not around Katie.

"Look, Jared?" Doubt edged her voice as she said his name, and Jared wondered if she'd flip-flop again on their date. She definitely seemed more on edge than yesterday morning, before Fred interrupted them. "I told you I wouldn't spy on Mandy for you, but—"

"I don't want you to. Really."

"Well, there's something I think you should know."

Jared set his hammer on top of the toolbox. "Is she all right?"

"Oh, yeah. She's fine." Katie's eyes crinkled at the corners. "But yesterday she came in after you left. I wasn't expecting her, or I'd have let you know."

Jared straightened from where he was kneeling, working on the new cabinets. "What happened?"

"She seemed out of it at first—well, let me rephrase. Not out of it. More like distracted. She asked to look at the design books again, but she kept looking at the pieces of the old countertop you'd stacked against the wall."

Jared frowned. "She knew I'd been here and that made her nervous?"

"Not exactly. She asked me how old the last cabinet was that you'd ripped out, and if I was excited to get a new one installed. Small talk. I mentioned that my grandfather had put in the original, and that I was sad to see it go, though I knew I needed a new one."

Katie shoved her hands in her pockets, looked away for a second, then looked back at Jared. "She asked me if family was important to me, and I replied that of course it is. My mother passed away long ago, but my dad and I are still close. I have dinner with him at least once a week, and we sometimes go to the movies together in Blair on the weekends. Apparently, it was the wrong thing to say."

"How so?"

Katie winced. "She said she's been thinking of trying to locate her mother. That now might be a good time, so she can try to get to know her mom before she and Kevin get married. Then she mentioned that maybe she could invite her mother to the wedding."

Jared couldn't have been more stunned if Katie had sucker punched him. He took a deep breath, trying to process the information. Corey coming to Bowen? It'd be disastrous.

"I'm sorry, Jared. I didn't realize that talking to Mandy about my family would spur her on. I just thought if she knew what a great relationship I had with my father, she'd see what a great father she has in you."

Katie took a step closer to him as she spoke. "I don't want to intrude in your personal life, but I'm under the impression you haven't spoken to Mandy's mother in years. I just thought you should be aware that Mandy might want to contact her."

"Yeah. Thanks." What could Mandy be thinking?

She *wasn't* thinking, he realized. She was dreaming. At an age where so many of Mandy's friends bickered constantly with their mothers, Mandy simply dreamed of meeting hers. She'd apparently decided—because it *felt* appropriate—that now would be a good time to try to touch base with a mother who'd never been involved in her life.

Problem was, no time would be right for Corey—he'd gone down that road. Corey knew exactly how to contact them whenever she wanted, and she'd stated flat-out that the part of her life she'd lived in Bowen was over, and that she had no desire to tread that ground again—either by her physical presence or by an emotional connection. She hadn't been mean about it; she was no ogre, just determined not to open old wounds.

"I told Mandy it might not be a good idea, since it was plain she hadn't mentioned her thoughts to you," Katie ventured. "She asked me why I disapproved, and I think she wanted to talk about it, but I already felt I'd gone too far, so I changed the subject. I'm just sorry it came up in the first place, or that I might have encouraged her. It wasn't my intention."

Jared smoothed a hand over his face, trying to wipe out his frustration. "I'm the one who should apologize, not you. I didn't mean to put you in this position. You didn't sign on to be a counselor as well as a wedding gown designer."

Katie gave him a sympathetic look. "Don't worry about it—you couldn't have known. But if she brings up the subject again, what would you like me to say?"

"You could tell her she should talk to me about it—" he chuckled aloud "—but I doubt that'd get a favorable reception."

Katie's face split into a grin. "Are you always able to laugh at yourself this way?"

"I try. Beats the alternative." He couldn't help but smile at Katie. She hardly knew him, yet she chose to see the best in him. That alone made him feel better—less rattled by the entire situation.

"She's going to bring it up again. It was obvious from the way she was acting with me she needs someone to talk to."

"Anyone but her father," he commented. He wasn't bitter about it. It was a fact of life for anyone raising a teen. And Mandy's opening up to Katie made sense, in a way. Katie was the only other person—well, besides Kevin—who knew she wanted to get married in the near future. "I don't know what to tell you. Play it by ear, I suppose."

"Okay."

She looked doubtful, so he explained, "Unfortunately, Cornelia—Mandy's mother—probably won't want to take a phone call from Mandy, let alone come to Bowen to visit."

"I see."

"Don't get me wrong, Corey's not a bad person. Really, she's not. But even if Corey does decide to talk to Mandy, it's not going to give Mandy whatever it is she's hoping for. If Mandy can learn that for herself, rather than having to hear it from her mother, I think that'd be better all around. I'd hate to see Mandy hurt."

Katie herself looked hurt, apparently imagining what it would feel like to receive a harsh phone call from one's own mother. "I'll gently dissuade her, then."

"Thank you. I really appreciate it." Heck, he appreciated that Katie had the fortitude to tell him about the incident in the first place.

She was about to duck back through the curtain, but he took a step forward and put a hand on her arm. "Don't judge Corey," he said. "Having a baby at eighteen changed her. It made her fearful. After Mandy was born, she needed to get away and start over, and I can't blame her. She lives a good life now. She knows I take good care of Mandy and that Mandy is a wonderful girl. She does care that her daughter's safe and sound, even if she's not the one taking care of her."

He wondered for a split second why he was so gung-ho to defend Corey to Katie, but at the expression of understanding on Katie's face, and the way the constriction in his throat instantly relaxed in response, he knew.

He didn't want Katie to judge him by Corey's behavior. He didn't want Katie to think less of him for being involved with Corey—no matter how long ago the relationship had been.

Katie lowered her eyes and slowly put her hand over his, then raised her chin just enough to met his gaze. "That's why you're so worried about Mandy getting married now. She might get pregnant."

"That's one concern. Mostly I dread the thought of her getting as overwhelmed as Corey did. Having a life-altering event happen at this age can be devastating, even if it's something that you think you want, like marriage. It can easily morph into a situation you're not ready to handle.''

For Corey it hadn't been the pregnancy that frightened and changed her so much as facing the crushing responsibility of raising a child—not to mention the concept of spending the rest of her life with him, when neither of them had a job or a college degree.

Katie nodded, then looked back down to where her hand covered his. For a moment he wondered if something similar had happened to her at eighteen when she left Bowen and went to Boston. It had been something she'd wanted—she'd said so herself. But was it a decision she'd come to regret? Had something triggered the same panic in her that Corey had experienced?

"You understand, don't you?"

"Nothing as drastic as what happened to you, but…'' Her hand tightened over his.

That was all it took. Before he could think about it, or analyze it, he bent and kissed her.

When she didn't pull away, he wrapped his other arm around her, pulling her closer, and brushed a second kiss against her lips. Her response was instant and nearly sent him to the floor.

As her mouth tensed, then relaxed against his, her hand fell away from his arm and snaked around his waist, knocking his tool belt loose. They ignored it, neither particularly concerned about the possibility of being scraped by the claw end of a hammer.

After a few more gentle, testing kisses, he eased

her a few steps backward, into her workroom, just out of sight of the glass door to the shop.

"In case Fred shows up," he explained. "No need to ruin your good reputation by being seen with a screw-up like me."

"I wondered if you were going to kiss me yesterday before he came in."

He kissed her once more, this time with a teasing smile playing at his lips. "It might've occurred to me."

A lazy, deliberate smile spread across her face in response. He noticed a glimmer of mischief flickering in the depths of her hazel eyes just before she placed her fingers on his cheeks and pulled his face back down to hers.

All was forgotten the moment her mouth opened beneath his. His hands tightened around her waist, and he fitted her body flush against his. Her fingers dropped to the front of his jeans, and for a split second he wondered how far and how fast the kiss would go. She twisted her hand between them, and his tool belt fell to the floor.

"Better," she murmured against his mouth, then snaked her arms up and around his neck.

He kissed her more deeply, wanting to get lost in the sensations—the clean smell of her hair, the baby-soft skin on her face, the warmth of her lips. He marveled at her passionate response to him and her ability to match his kisses move for move.

Was she as hungry for this as he had been? It

seemed so, which surprised him and thrilled him at the same time. He lost track of time as they stood near the curtained door to the workroom, kissing each other, exploring each other with slow caresses.

When he felt his knees might give, he leaned forward, gradually pushing her toward the oversize worktable. With one motion, he lifted her onto an empty spot. One of her legs wrapped around his, and she pulled him down, so his body stayed in contact with hers.

"Hope this is a sturdy table," he said, half serious.

"Hope so, too." She smiled, then kissed him again. Her hands lingered near his waist, then ran upward, her fingernails trailing along his back, nearly sending him over the edge with each stroke.

He could close his eyes and let her do that all day. Damn, but it had been way, way too long. Had his body felt so on fire before? He couldn't recall.

He exhaled as her fingers tangled in his hair, and he dipped his head to kiss her neck, her jawline, then the small space behind her ear where her jaw ended and her hairline began. A soft sigh escaped her lips and she shifted under him. He savored the way the contours of her breasts pushed against his chest, and at the thought of what they'd be doing in a few more minutes if they kept up like they were, he nearly exploded.

They hadn't even made it to Celestino's for their first date yet.

He wondered what, exactly, he wanted from her.

Certainly he wanted to make love to her—his body screamed for it. He knew sharing a bed with Katie, watching as she tilted her head back at that final moment, maybe calling his name with her blond hair splayed across his navy blue sheets, would be flat-out fantastic.

But what did he *really* want from Katie, for the long term? After all this time, was he ready for a relationship that might go past a few casual dates?

If he made love to her, it couldn't be a one-night stand—he'd never been wired that way, and he had the feeling Katie wasn't, either. He was kissing her in a room filled with wedding gowns, for crying out loud. But was he ready for the kind of emotional step it'd take to have someone other than Mandy in his home, sitting down with him to dinner or discussing the morning paper over coffee?

And if he was willing to take that step—to finally pursue a relationship with a woman—was Katie the right woman? She'd turned him down once. There had to be a reason, a reason she'd pushed aside today.

"So," she whispered close to his ear, "if this is what I get when you come over to install cabinets, what happens after Celestino's?"

He propped himself up on his elbows, moving so his forehead rested on hers to give them a slight distance, but so he could still feel the length of her body along his own.

If he had any sense at all, he'd just kiss her and keep going.

"I was wondering the same thing," he admitted with a wry grin. "I hadn't thought that far ahead. Of course, I hadn't thought..." He wrapped his finger around a lock of her hair, playing with it for a moment before letting it fall back to her cheek, and she flushed in response.

"No, me, either."

Reluctantly, he eased back off the table and offered Katie a hand to pull her up to sitting. They'd both reached that awkward point—where they either needed to go forward full tilt, or pull back and be reasonable.

Reason won out. "At least Fred didn't show."

"I knew we'd be safe for another hour or so," she said.

"So you *were* thinking ahead."

Her laughter filled the small workroom. "Well, I can imagine all kinds of things." She stood, still holding his hand, unwilling to let go just yet. Her expression suddenly serious, she met his gaze and said, "There's something to this, I think."

"I think so, too."

"I'm not the type who does this very often. Well, not at all since I got back to Bowen, if you want to know the truth, which you probably don't." She worried her lip, apparently knowing that her words were coming out too fast and without thought.

He cupped her chin, raised it so she wouldn't look away, so she could see this was no casual encounter for him, either. "I want to know all about you. Everything. I just don't know if I'm ready for it. Because I'm not the type who does this very often, either. For a number of reasons.''

Well, two reasons. Mandy, obviously, and Corey. He'd never gotten over the fact Corey didn't believe in him, and he needed to know that Katie could before he let himself even think of getting involved.

She gave a slight nod, and he bent and kissed her again, though this time it was barely a brushing of the lips.

''I'd still like to go to Celestino's on Friday,'' he said, ''but only if you're up for it.''

She hesitated, so he let go of her chin. He glanced over his shoulder toward the main room. ''Look, I'm nearly finished with what I wanted to do today on the cabinets. Why don't I knock off for the day. It might be easier to think if we're not both in the same two hundred square feet of space. I should probably clean up first—''

''Nah, don't worry about it. No one's going to be out there today.''

Probably true. And if he took too long straightening, he'd end up trying to get back behind the curtain again to continue what they started. His brain would formulate some excuse, despite the fact they both needed time to process what was happening between them. ''All right. I'll be back tomorrow. You can tell me to take a hike then, if you like.

''I wouldn't tell you to take a hike.''

''Not before I finish the cabinets, at least.''

That elicited another of her megawatt grins. "You're a very funny guy, Jared Porter."

Funny wasn't necessarily the way he'd want her to describe him, given their afternoon together. "As long as I leave you with a smile on your face, I guess that's good enough."

For now.

Chapter Six

"He's never this messy at home, really."

Mandy wrinkled her nose as she examined the dusty floor of The Bowen Bride. She stepped gingerly around the cabinet frame her father and her uncle had carried in that morning, then spread her hands wide, as if pleading a case in court. "I swear he's not. He even does the dishes before he goes to bed instead of letting them soak overnight, and he uses the good kind of laundry detergent to make his colors brighter and his whites whiter."

"It's okay, Mandy, you can come back here to look at the design books," Katie couldn't hide her amusement as she waved the teen into her workroom. She hadn't been expecting Mandy to stop by, but she wasn't entirely surprised when the teen called from her cell phone to say she was on her way over, either.

It figured she'd come over after she knew her father would be gone for the day.

"It's not that messy," she told Mandy. "Besides, only a couple more days and he'll be out of here. And when he's finished, I'll have a very nice new counter with cabinets made to order."

And who knew what else she'd have. A man in her life for the first time since she'd returned to Bowen? A bushel of doubts and fears, all brought to the surface again? Worries about trying to live up to someone else's expectations?

Or would she be stuck with a serious case of lust that wasn't going to be satisfied in one afternoon? Kissing Jared had taught her that that, at least, was a given. If she closed her eyes, she could still imagine the way his skin warmed her fingertips even through his T-shirt.

She'd worked through the early afternoon with his freshly soaped scent still teasing her senses. As she'd cut the fabric on a gown for a bride-to-be from the nearby town of Tekamah, he'd invaded her daydreams and ratcheted them to an instant R rating. She'd come close to making a mistake with her scissors more than once.

"Wow, look at all this," Mandy breathed as she entered the workroom and surveyed the bolts of silk, taffeta and satin lining the walls. "It really *is* magical back here. Cinderella's fairy godmother probably couldn't even come up with this many choices of fabric and lace."

Katie said a polite thank-you, not wanting Mandy to dwell on whether or not the shop was truly magical, and set the design books at one end of the worktable for Mandy to peruse. Then she pulled out a legal pad to take notes. "You said you'd settled on a few things?"

Mandy's face broke into a broad smile. "Yeah. Kevin and I were out shopping and I tried to get his opinion, but in a backward sort of way, you know? I wanted to find out what he likes, but I didn't want him to know what I'm actually going to get. I think that'd be bad luck. So I kept commenting on pictures of wedding gowns worn by actresses on the front of the *National Enquirer* and all the other magazines at checkout."

"And did he have an opinion?"

"Not really. Though I did eliminate some ideas. He hated anything that was too poofy. That was his one big thing."

"No poof, no problem. Though if you're paging through the books and see a dress you like but are tempted to eliminate it simply because it's too poofy, let me know. I can usually take poof down a notch."

"Actually, I already know what I want." Mandy flipped open the largest of the design books, then scoured the pages for a moment.

"This one," she said, spinning the book around. "I saw this last time I was here. I really like the way the top is fitted. It's graceful, plus it'll cover the fact I'm not totally stacked. And I like the bottom of the one on the next page. Is there some way I can combine the two? I think it'd have a vintage look—like a classy Hollywood gown from the forties or fifties, you know?''

Katie studied both gowns. ''I have an idea.'' She circled the worktable and grabbed another book, then opened it about midway, to a photograph of a gown her grandmother had designed. It had always been one of her favorites—something she'd wear, if she ever did decide to get married. ''What do you think of this?''

''Oh, wow. Yeah.'' Tears welled in Mandy's eyes. ''That's totally what I had in my head. Totally. Do you think Kevin will like it?''

''I don't exactly know Kevin's taste,'' Katie admitted. ''But judging from your reaction, I bet he would.''

''Then that's what I want. I'm positive.'' She looked from the book to Katie. ''We're talking about getting married right after graduation—the first week of June. Is that enough time? I mean, a bridal magazine I read said gowns can take nine months or more.''

''That's plenty of time for me. Don't worry. In fact, it might be better if I hold off starting the gown for a couple months until, say, after Christmas. That'll keep you from being locked in if you change your mind about what you want.''

Mandy nodded, and Katie wondered if she caught the double meaning, that in time she might change her mind about the dress—or about the wedding itself.

Katie marked the page, then made a few notes on her pad while Mandy continued to stare at the picture. "I know you never knew her, but…"

Katie glanced up, afraid of what was coming next. "Knew who?"

"Do you think it's the kind of gown my mother would like? I feel like I should have something she'd approve of."

"I'm sure she would, if she had an opinion. It's a classic design and in a cut that'll flatter your figure."

Mandy fiddled with the corner of the page. "Yeah. I just wish I knew for sure. If she decides to come, I want to look perfect."

Katie set down her pen and tried to think of how Jared would have her handle the topic. "Mandy, it's my understanding you've never actually met your mother."

The teen shook her head. "She moved to Chicago when I was three weeks old. She hasn't seen me since then, or even talked to me, but she talks to my dad once a year or so to check on how I'm doing."

Katie could see how it hurt Mandy to admit her mother had never even spoken to her. "It's probably hard, not having your mom around."

"It completely sucks." A sigh escaped her, and she let go of the page. "None of my friends get it. They actually think it'd be cool to only have to get their dad's permission to do something. Or to be able to have the whole house to yourself after school, because there's no mother there and your dad's still at work. They even say stuff like, 'It's not like you knew her and she died or anything.' I mean, I'm sure that would make it harder, but puh-leeze.''

"I know the feeling," Katie replied. "My mother died when I was very young—not even a year old—and my dad never remarried. My friends made similar comments.''

Careful in her choice of words, Katie explained, "I'm sure it's even harder for you. You know your mother is out there, somewhere, and it makes you wonder. I never had to deal with that—with having to set aside someone who was alive but not around. But I always used to wonder what my life would have been like if she'd been around. Whether I would have been more confident, for instance. Or if I still would have gone away to college, or just stayed put. All the what-ifs.''

"I do wonder. All the time," Mandy admitted. "I probably shouldn't, but I do.''

"I think it's natural." Katie leaned back in her chair, trying to keep her tone casual, while still getting the message through to Mandy. "And I don't know about you, but not having a mom around made me realize how much my friends took their mothers for granted. They might've argued more with their moms than with their dads, and sometimes griped about how strict their moms could be, but they always had someone they could talk with about girl things. It's not the same with a father.''

Mandy rolled her eyes. "No kidding. I love my dad, but like, I could never talk to him about Kevin. Not about anything too deep. It'd be bizarro. He just doesn't get what it's like to be a female. Last year I put highlights in my hair before junior prom, and my dad hit the freakin' roof. I mean, come *on*. It was just highlights. If my mom had been around, she'd have probably taken me to the salon herself.''

Mandy let out a little snort. "If he's going to go berserk over something silly like highlights, imagine what he'd think if I tried to talk to him about stuff at school or about my relationship with Kevin. But a mom would talk about those things. Well, as long as I didn't go into too much detail, if you know what I mean.''

"That's probably true.'' Katie smiled, then took a deep breath before plunging ahead. "On the other hand, you're pretty lucky to have the dad you have. When you look at your friends and realize how much they take their mothers for granted, do you ever wonder if you take your father for granted? All the hard work he does to give you a good home, or all the love he's given you?''

"Yeah. I probably *should* be more grateful. But it's hard, you know?''

"Believe me, I do.'' Katie took a long sip of the soda she'd pulled from the fridge before Mandy came over. "It sounds like you know very little about your mother. What does your father think about you calling her?''

"He's never let me call her before when I've asked, so I didn't tell him I want to now.'' She shrugged. "I figure I'm old enough to call her without asking his permission. I can talk to her adult to adult now. And it's not like I'm going to ask her to take care of me or send me money or anything. I just want to get to know her, and for her to get to know me. No expectations.''

Mandy had a point. In less than a year, she would be on her own, but she definitely harbored expectations.

"Maybe so," Katie replied. "But that still doesn't mean you should. No matter how old you get, there are some things you should always talk to your parents about—especially a parent like your father, who you love and you're grateful for. Contacting someone from their past is one of those things. You wouldn't contact your best friend's ex-boyfriend without talking to her about it first, would you?''

"I hadn't thought about it that way, I guess.'' Mandy glanced at the book, an uncomfortable look on her face. "Well, that stinks.''

"You already called her? Or wrote to her?''

The color rose on Mandy's neck and cheeks, and she looked down at her hands. "Yeah. I did an Internet search and found her phone number. She's in Downers Grove, a suburb of Chicago. I tried calling a few times. There was never an answer, so I finally left a message last night with my cell number. I didn't tell her what it was about—just to call me. But she hasn't.''

Katie put her hand over Mandy's, her heart aching in sympathy. She'd only known Mandy a few days, but already she'd become attached to the teen. Jared was just as fortunate to have such a wonderful daughter as the girl was to have him as her father. ''I know this probably isn't the best advice, but try to put it out of your mind. And try not to be hurt if she doesn't call you. She doesn't know you, Mandy. She only knows your father, and maybe that relationship is a painful memory for her, something she can't bring herself to face.''

''Calling was probably the wrong move.''

''Well, it's done now, so no sense in dwelling on it. If she calls back, you can feel her out. But take it slowly. And consider telling your father that you called her. He might be willing to open up a little about her and tell you whether it's a good idea to let her know you and Kevin plan to get married.''

''You really think I should?'' Mandy's eyes widened. ''You don't think he'll just get mad? He's already ticked off at me because I want to get married.''

Katie squeezed Mandy's hand. ''He might be angry at first, but I think he'd really want to know. And I bet, if you give him a chance, he'll listen to how you really feel.'' At least, Katie hoped so. Otherwise he'd likely be angry with *her* for giving Mandy lousy advice.

The wall phone in the workroom rang, and Katie shot Mandy a reassuring smile as she pushed back from the table to answer it. Mandy hoisted her backpack over one shoulder and signaled an *Are we done?* as Katie stretched across a countertop to reach the phone.

"The Bowen Bride," she answered on the third ring. She nodded to Mandy, who closed the design books and started organizing them into a pile at one end of the table.

"Katie, it's Jared."

The even, slow thrum of her heartbeat instantly revved into overdrive. Keeping a businesslike tone, she replied, "Yes, what can I do for you?"

His voice dropped. "Mandy's there. Is she in the workroom? Right now?"

"Yes. Did you need to stop by?"

"I left my tool belt. Have you seen it? Or has she?"

Katie's gaze slid to the floor. As nonchalantly as possible, she scanned the area near the door, then looked toward the table until she saw the tan leather belt. She—or Jared—must have kicked it under the worktable at some point after she'd unhooked it from his waist. Hammer, nails bags, and all.

"No, she hasn't yet, but I'll take care of it."

Thank goodness. There'd be no reason in the world for her father's tool belt to be in the workroom, let alone dropped haphazardly under the table with the tape measure falling out of its designated pocket.

Mandy wasn't as naive as Fred Winston, either. If she spotted it, she'd add up the evidence and figure out what had happened.

"Well, it's probably a bad idea for me to get it now. Shoot." He mumbled something else under his breath. "She's going over to a friend's with Kevin tonight. There's a television show they all watch together on Wednesdays whenever she's not baby-sitting for the Winstons, and I'm pretty sure Fred didn't need her tonight. She doesn't have to be home until nine-thirty. Would it be possible for you to run it by my place before then?"

"I can do that, sure." Katie eyed Mandy, who had one foot on the chair she'd just occupied, tying her shoelace before heading out the door. "Though the situation here may change shortly."

"Our house is the left turn before you get to the Eberhardt place. You know where it is?"

She mentally pictured the correct turn off the highway. "Yes, I think so. I'll see you then."

"Okay. Call if you need directions. The driveway's easy to miss."

"I will. Bye."

Mandy finished tying her shoe, then shot a pointed look at the phone as she waved a goodbye to Katie. "Sounds like you've got a lot of customers."

"Nothing out of the ordinary." Well, not if it had actually been a business call. "I'll see you soon, Mandy."

After Mandy walked out, Katie leaned against the

door frame for a moment with the workroom at her back, gathering her thoughts. A pickup zoomed by on Main Street, followed by the sheriff's white sedan. She grinned to herself, shook her head, then turned and fished the tool belt out from under the table. Just in case Mandy—or anyone else—came back in the workroom, she placed it on an empty shelf in a workroom closet she hardly used.

The clock on the wall read four-thirty. Pretty soon everyone would be knocking off for the evening and Main Street would quiet down. She should call her supplier in Omaha before he left for the evening and check on some buttons she'd special-ordered. Should. But something in the closet caught her eye, and now her brain processed what she'd seen.

Turning around, she opened the closet door and crouched down to take a second look at the bottom shelves. There, at ankle level, were two sagging cardboard boxes labeled Accounts in her Oma's handwriting. How had she not noticed these before? Or maybe she had when she'd first moved into the space, but hadn't paid attention.

She thought of Mandy, glanced over at the thread on her pegboard, then back at the boxes. She put her elbows on her knees and puffed out a breath, debating.

She had to know for sure.

Leaning forward on her hands and knees, she pulled the two dusty boxes from their shelves, lifted them onto the table, flipped the cardboard lid off one, then sat down to read.

When the doorbell finally rang a little after seven, Jared was halfway through his third cup of coffee. He swigged the last drops, trying to remember if he'd brewed regular or decaf.

Not that it'd make a bit of difference. He couldn't imagine falling asleep easily tonight.

He set the Bowen Railroaders coffee mug—a gift from Mandy—in the sink. After wiping his hands on a towel, he strode to the door, pausing for a beat before grabbing the knob, unsure whether to say hello, take the tool belt and say goodbye all in one breath—or to invite her in for a cup of coffee.

And then there was the third option—to grab her and kiss her senseless before his brain realized the idiocy of it all.

When he opened the door and saw her, blond hair shining under the porch light, his fingers twitched, and he held them tight to his sides for a beat. Every fiber in his body ached to go for option three.

"Hi." The night was warm, but she had her arms wrapped around her. "I hope you don't mind, but I left the belt in my car until I was sure the coast was clear."

He pushed open the screen door and held it with his hip. "It's fine. Mandy's at a friend's. Though she probably wouldn't have thought anything of it."

One side of Katie's mouth curved up. "How many

times have you left your tool belt behind on a job site?''

"Once."

"Today?"

"Yep." And then he did the stupidest thing of all. He bent forward, put his hands on either side of her head and kissed her. No one could see his front porch—the neighbor's cornfields blocked the view of any passersby on the dirt road and the Eberhardts' house was nearly a half mile away, on the opposite side of their fields. But it felt daring, as if he'd just taken a bungee jump off a high tower without first checking the bungee cord to be certain it was properly attached.

His younger self—the one who'd whooped it up and partied his way through high school—would've laughed himself into a state at the thought of a moonlight kiss being daring. Especially since he was now an adult, and a completely unattached one, at that.

Katie returned his kiss, sending an instant shot of warmth through him. Her fingers reached up to cover his as she took a step forward into him, molding her body to his in a way that made him want to pull her indoors and onto the sofa before either of them could change their minds.

But almost before the kiss began, she dropped her hands to his chest, then leaned her forehead against his shoulder and exhaled. "Whoa."

Whoa, indeed. He could think of a few other choice phrases.

"I know this is a sentence that every man dreads hearing, but we really need to talk."

He buried his face in her soft blond hair. She knew—had to know—what existed between them wasn't an everyday attraction. They both thrummed with it. If what either one wanted was a casual romp, they could have found that in Bowen anytime. He'd avoided it for obvious reasons, and wondered what had held her back. Given her behavior the last few days, and the fact he hadn't heard any talk about her, he didn't imagine she'd been involved with anyone local.

Clearly, they each wanted something else.

"Yeah," he mumbled near her ear. "We probably should talk."

He let go of her reluctantly, then gestured to the far end of the porch, where a white swing hung from two chains and a single slatted rocking chair creaked in the evening air. She hesitated for a moment, then took a seat in the rocker Mandy favored.

"It's beautiful out here," she commented, staring out past the porch rail. "Is that the Eberhardts' corn-field at the edge of your front yard, or yours?"

"Eberhardts'."

"Good neighbors, I bet. Carolyn Eberhardt's mother was good friends with my grandmother. She managed the funeral arrangements for my grand-mother when Opa passed. She was fabulous that way."

The motion-sensing light that had turned on in the

driveway when she approached clicked off, casting the porch in semidarkness. He realized he'd forgotten to turn on the porch light, but he could just make out her features in the light glowing from behind the curtains in his front windows.

"Yeah, they're great. Used to baby-sit Mandy for me, back when she was really little and I could barely afford to pay them." He didn't want to talk about the Eberhardts, though, and figured she hadn't broken off their kiss to discuss the neighbors, either.

"So tell me," he began, "why'd you originally turn me down for the date?" Because it was patently obvious to them both that chemistry had nothing to do with it. "Whatever the reason, it was pretty important to you."

He glanced at his battered truck, parked next to her shiny, late-model Volkswagen. Once again he wondered if maybe it was an education thing. He'd never attended college, whereas she'd obtained her degree. She'd opened her own successful business, while he still worked for his younger brother.

Or maybe she was just freaked out that he was the father of a seventeen-year-old. Many fathers his age were just getting their kids potty trained or starting to teach them basic addition.

She leaned forward in the rocker. "You just cut right to the heart of it, don't you?"

"No sense in doing otherwise. I take it that's what you wanted to talk about?"

If she was going to tell him they weren't right for

each other, that their backgrounds were too dissimilar, he wanted it up front. Katie didn't seem the judgmental type, but then again, Corey hadn't seemed the type to bolt when the going got tough.

"Actually, no. Though at some point I suppose we should talk about that."

"Ah. So it's me." He forced himself to crack a smile. "Well, I apologize if I'm a rotten kisser, then."

Chapter Seven

"**W**ell, that's not a problem, either." Katie's voice was low as she added, "I mean, you're not terrible, and I think you know it."

"Good to hear it, anyway."

If it'd been noon instead of evening, he was certain he would see her flush, but her voice was level as she continued, "I actually wanted to talk about Mandy."

Mandy? So much for the temporary thrill at discovering she enjoyed their kisses as much as he did. "Thought we did that this afternoon."

He raised an eyebrow, not that she could see him very well. But despite the darkness, he wasn't sure he should invite her inside, not until he figured out what gnawed at her and whether or not she wanted to be invited in.

"This is something new."

"Okay, then shoot."

He wondered if she knew that Mandy was the one thing keeping him from going full tilt after a relationship with her—would it be the right thing to do, to pursue a serious relationship—when Mandy was having relationship issues of her own? And would he be able to mentally let go and enjoy himself, as he had been unable to do since Mandy's birth?

He was willing to try—with Katie more than with anyone he'd ever met—but that was no guarantee a relationship between them would work, even though she did make his body react with the fierce drive of an adolescent.

"I don't want to violate her confidence, but she's already called her mother. She told me this afternoon that she left a message and hasn't heard back."

"I can't believe—"

Anger and a sense of betrayal flared in him, though logic told him that Mandy's actions had nothing to do with him or her relationship with him.

"I think she regrets it already. I just wanted to give you a heads-up." Katie bit her lip. In the moonlight, he could see sympathy and worry mixing in her expression. "She's planning to tell you about it, but she's afraid that when she does you'll be angry with her. Don't be. She's at an age where being without a mother is tough—and it has nothing to do with wanting her mother around at the wedding if she marries Kevin. Seventeen is hard, no matter what."

He dropped into the porch swing and stared out

into the night. "I won't be angry with her." Well, at least he wouldn't tell Mandy he was angry. "I know better than anyone how hard seventeen can be. But thanks for the warning."

As the light of the moon illuminated the whisper-thin clouds skittering overhead, a sudden memory popped into Jared's head. He could picture Mandy, as clearly as if it'd occurred yesterday, flashlight under her bed sheets at two in the morning, reading to herself on an early autumn evening much like this one.

She'd been six years old at the most. She was still reading aloud to herself and sounding out each word syllable by syllable. Though he probably should have told her to go to sleep, he'd simply backed out of her room and into the hall, listening through the open door as she whispered about Curious George and his adventures with the Man in the Yellow Hat. His heart had been so full of love, watching the circle of light as it shone through the thin sheet.

"She's almost grown up, in many ways." Katie's voice was as soft as the moonlit clouds overhead.

"So she tells me."

"But she's not there yet. She knows it, in her heart, and she'll realize it. You survived being a teenager under adverse circumstances. So will she. And I have a feeling you had it a heck of a lot worse than Mandy."

Jared hazarded a glance at Katie, and she reached across the space between the rocker and the swing to put her hand over his. "She's a smart girl, Jared, and a kind girl. You've raised her well under what had to be very difficult circumstances. You should be proud of yourself and proud of her."

He spread his fingers, reaching out across the space between the swing and the rocker, then pulling the rocker a little closer and wending his fingers in between hers so she couldn't withdraw.

How did women do all the things they did with such small, delicate fingers?

"I only vaguely remember Mandy's mother," Katie said after they'd sat in silence for a while. "You two dated your entire senior year, didn't you?"

Was this the other reason she needed to talk? He looked down at Katie's hand in his. She didn't yank it away, so he assumed she was fine with the contact. "We started going out our junior year of high school, then through senior year."

"And she got pregnant."

"An accident, as you probably guessed."

"But you didn't get married? I get the impression you wanted to get married but she didn't."

Jared shook his head. He'd never talked about it— not since he was eighteen and tried to hash out the whole situation with his parents, who'd cried, then yelled, then cried some more. But the way Katie approached it, he didn't mind the subject. She wasn't one of the town busybodies, either trying to gather gossip or pass judgment on him. She asked because she cared.

"You wanted to, didn't you?"

He let out a half laugh. "Wanted to and dismissed the idea almost immediately. Corey told me she was pregnant and that she didn't want to get married in a practiced speech that lasted all of two minutes. I was shocked as much by her desire not to marry me as I was by the pregnancy."

He swallowed hard, then tightened his fingers around Katie's for a moment. "Don't get me wrong— I was no saint. I loved her as much as I was capable of loving someone back then, but marriage wasn't even on my radar screen. I'd been accepted to a couple small colleges and figured that's where I was headed—with or without Corey. But when she looked at me and said she was pregnant with my child, I instantly knew we had to get married. It was the proper thing to do. Even though I was stupid and got her pregnant, I was raised with very traditional values. You marry the mother of your children, and you take care of her and respect her, no matter what."

"But she didn't want to?"

"No. And if I had gone ahead and proposed, tried to get her to change her mind about marriage—which I know she wouldn't have done—it would have ended in divorce. She wouldn't have stayed with me for long. I have no illusions about that. She wanted to move on to bigger and better things."

Things like life in a big city and all the perks that went with it. Movie theaters showing a dozen films at once. Restaurants and coffee shops on every street corner. Places to go dancing, museums to explore, professional sporting events to attend.

Corey hadn't planned to spend her life tied to a husband in Bowen, Nebraska, living in a house her husband built himself on open land behind the Eberhardts' cornfield, eight miles from the nearest one-screen movie theater and more than an hour from the nearest megamall.

"You sound awfully matter-of-fact about it."

He shrugged. "It's the truth. And it was seventeen years ago. A lot can happen in seventeen years—you can even learn to forgive yourself. I'm a completely different person than I was then, and I'm sure Corey is, too."

"Mandy says she's living in the Chicago suburbs."

"Probably. She's lived in an apartment in town for years, near Navy Pier, but last time we talked—about a year ago—she mentioned that she was house hunting. I think she might be married, but I'm not sure. If she is, she kept her maiden name. But it's not something we've talked about."

"I see."

"She's been in Chicago ever since she left Bowen. She's made a good life for herself there. Of course, her parents wanted to kill me. First for getting her pregnant, then for not marrying her. When she moved away, it was the last straw. You were probably in college by the time her parents left town. It wasn't pretty. They made sure all their friends knew how angry they were with me before they moved."

"I'm so sorry, Jared."

"You know, it sounds awful when I explain it now, but in reality, it's all turned out all right." He turned to face Katie, his eyes straining in the darkness. He wanted to erase her doubts, to assure her that any relationship he had with Corey was way back in the past. Ancient history.

"What happened was right, in the end, both for me and for Corey. I have no regrets. Of course, that doesn't mean I'd do it all over again, either."

Katie was kind enough to laugh. "No, I imagine not."

"I just hope this whole crazy marriage idea works out for Mandy. You said it yourself—she's a great kid. Very smart and responsible. Since it's always been just the two of us, she's had to be. But in a lot of ways she's still growing into the woman I know she'll become. She needs space to grow and change, and if she gets married now..."

He let the thought drift into the night air. Though Katie didn't say anything, he knew she understood. That alone lifted the weight of worry from his shoulders.

"But what about you, Jared? What's the right thing for you now?"

"I'm not certain." His heart was telling him that Katie could be the right thing—if she wanted him.

It felt so natural, sitting on the front porch under the stars, talking with her while the crickets made their nightly racket and the cornstalks rustled in the breeze. "But I wonder if it might be you. I've never even had a 'maybe' thought in that direction before. Never met a woman I connected with so quickly."

Where'd that come from? You didn't tell a woman something like that unless you were willing to back it up, and they hardly knew each other.

Only enough to know their backgrounds were as dissimilar as they were similar.

He glanced toward the screen door, noticing a dark shape pressing against the mesh. Suddenly needing the distraction—had he just hung himself out on a limb or what?—he called out, "C'mon, Scout."

He waved the dog out and stomped his foot on the porch, making the planks vibrate. He explained, "Scout's beyond old. Deaf as can be and completely harmless. So if you're afraid of dogs, don't be."

"I'm not," Katie replied, extending her hand so the German shepherd, who'd nosed his way through the door at the invitation from his owner, could sniff it and discover she posed him no threat.

"So is that what you wanted to talk about?" he asked. "I was expecting something completely unrelated to Corey or to my daughter or her current bout of teen angst."

Like why Katie had initially shied away from going out to dinner. He couldn't see a single reason why someone like Katie—young, beautiful, successful, and apparently available—would fear going on a date with him. Especially since she changed her mind so soon afterward and accepted his invitation.

"Well, it is about Mandy, in a way. But also about us." She seemed to swallow the word *us* as she said it, as if worried that using the term would make it a reality she wasn't ready to pursue.

Yep, he'd definitely blown it.

He should have kept his mouth shut until he knew where he really stood with her. Maybe nothing would come of a relationship between them, but he'd at least wanted to keep the possibility open. Not blow it before it even got off the ground.

Scout rubbed his back against the side of Katie's rocking chair, then put his head in Katie's lap, apparently deciding she'd pass muster. Katie smiled, then gently withdrew her hand from Jared's to reach down and stroke the dog's head with both hands.

He wondered if it was an excuse to break their contact, a desire to appease Scout, or because she felt the need to draw courage from the affectionate dog.

"You mentioned that Mandy read the article about The Bowen Bride in the *Gazette*."

He nodded, but she didn't respond. He wondered if she had difficulty seeing him in the moonlight, so he added, "She saw it."

A sigh escaped her, barely audible even from just an arm's length away in the September night. "Well, I know it sounds farfetched—that everyone who wears one of my gowns stays married forever—but as far as I know it's true."

What was she getting at? He leaned back in the swing and stretched his legs. "Doesn't surprise me.

Bowen doesn't exactly have the highest divorce rate in the country. Most people here get married to someone they've known since birth. They know the person pretty well before they say their I do's.''

"It's not just Bowen. It's every dress ever made in the shop. Every dress my grandmother ever made. I've gone through her records— I actually spent this afternoon going through them to be sure—and every single couple is still together. Well—'' she let out a small laugh ''—except for the dead ones. My grandmother's long gone and so are quite a few of her clients. But not one of those, to my knowledge, ever divorced or separated from their spouse.''

She sounded distressed by that fact. "It's a little hard to believe there were no divorces at all, but isn't that a good thing when couples stay married?''

"I don't know. I mean, some couples don't belong together. It's just a fact of life.'' He could almost hear her unspoken thought. *Couples like you and Corey.*

He pushed against the porch with his feet, giving the swing a gentle rock backward. "I agree. But you're telling me you think that just because you make a woman's dress, that's the reason her marriage hangs together? Not to crush your ego or disparage your skill as a dressmaker, but I'm guessing that's not the main reason.''

The right wedding gown didn't even enter into the equation. A woman could wear a rucksack when she walked down the aisle if the couple loved, respected, and honored one another. Wouldn't make a bit of difference to the marriage. Certainly the pricey designer gowns worn by many Hollywood brides hadn't helped their marriages click.

"I never thought so, either." Scout let out a low, contented growl as Katie kneaded the fur between the dog's ears with more pressure. "My grandmother mentioned it to me once, saying that no one who wore one of her gowns ever divorced, though I'm not sure that's exactly how she phrased it. I tucked that statement away as simply one more of my grandmother's stories. Oma was always a big storyteller."

"I suspect your grandmother had a lot of stories to tell."

He remembered the Schmidts. Once, as a child, he'd sat on his father's shoulders to watch Katie's grandparents lead the town's Fourth of July parade right down Main Street. In Bowen, to lead the parade was a huge honor. "When I was a kid, everyone knew who she was. Your grandfather, too. They were very involved in the community. Knew everyone and everything that went on."

She let out a puff of air. "True. But after that article ran in the *Gazette,* I started to wonder if it really was just another of her tall tales. At first I thought the reporter who came to my shop wanting to do a story was just trying to fill his pages for the next issue. You know, run a profile of a local business since there were no athletics to cover with school still out for the summer."

Jared grinned in the darkness. "I figured you'd

handed the reporter a press release or sent over your business card and flyers, like every other Bowen business does.''

''No. At least, I haven't done it since I opened my shop a few years back, and even then, I certainly didn't mention my grandmother's claim. But here's the weird part. The reporter told me his mother's gown had come from The Bowen Bride, back when it was Oma's shop, and his mother told him the same story my grandmother told me.'' Her hand stilled over Scout's head, and she glanced at him. ''Don't you find that a little odd?''

''That your grandmother told his mother if she bought a gown there, it guaranteed a long marriage?''

''More than that. My grandmother claimed that each gown leaving her shop was, for lack of a better term, magic. And this reporter said his mother believed it wholeheartedly.''

''Magic? Are you serious?''

''Absolutely. And so was the reporter.''

He tried not to laugh. Brides in magic gowns? In *Nebraska?* What next, enchanted corsages from fairy godmothers? Aliens conducting weddings on the town common?

The *Gazette* wasn't the *New York Times,* but it was no supermarket tabloid, either.

''That's, uh, hard to believe.''

''I know. But that's apparently why couples stay together. The magic. Remember the old spool of thread you saw in my shop this afternoon? It's in the hem of every gown I sew. I only use it because my grandmother did, and it makes me feel good to do it. But she told me she used it specifically because of its magic. Though for the life of me I wish I could remember her exact words.''

''What'd you tell the guy from the *Gazette?*''

''Nothing.'' She shrugged. ''I didn't mention the thread to the reporter because, frankly, I didn't believe the whole no-couple-ever-divorces bit was anything other than coincidence made to seem more important by my grandmother's wild tale. I just nodded along when he told me his mother's story. And I didn't contradict him on the statistics because, for one, I couldn't think of anyone who'd divorced off the top of my head, and second, a rumor like that floating around can be extremely good for business.''

''And now?''

She looked up from Scout and met Jared's gaze straight on. A mixture of concern and worry flickered in her eyes, her emotions so apparent he could read them even in the semidarkness of the front porch.

''Now I'm beginning to think his story—my grandmother's story—might actually be true. And that's a big problem.''

Jared couldn't believe his ears. She was completely, one hundred percent, serious.

This was why she wouldn't finish the kiss they'd started when she arrived? If she had some problem with dating a single father, fine. Concerns their professional and educational backgrounds were too divergent? Completely understandable. But magic wedding gowns?

Maybe she wasn't as into him as her kisses indicated. Or she was being polite about his I'm-a-rotten-kisser teasing.

Or maybe he just couldn't read women anymore.

He straightened in the swing, trying to process her logic. "Setting aside the ludicrous idea that couples staying married poses a major societal problem, you're telling me you honestly believe you're making dresses with magic thread. No offense, Katie, but that's insane."

"I agree!" She spread her hands wide as she spoke, causing Scout to raise his head off her lap in surprise. "Do I look like the type who goes for the supernatural mumbo-jumbo? I'm a practical person. But when you go through hundreds of records and you know most of the couples—and in some cases their children and grandchildren—and then you look up the others in the phone book—"

"You looked up your grandmother's clients in the phone book?"

"Well, on the Internet, if they weren't in the local phone directory. I found as many as I could. Most are in Blair, Tekamah, Herman, Macy and Fort Calhoun—" she ticked off the small towns on her fingers as she spoke "—but I even found a few listed in Omaha, Lincoln, and Sioux Falls."

"This is unreal—"

"It didn't take me as long as it sounds. No one

around here seems to move very often, and everyone I could find was listed as Mr. and Mrs. in the latest phone book. Don't you find that unreal? I don't want to believe it, but with today's divorce rate, the odds of *all* those couples staying together must be astronomical.''

He ran his hands over his blue jean-clad knees and stared out past the porch rail, toward the long rows of corn rustling in the night wind, lit by the stars and moon above. He loved this view—peaceful, quiet, easy. It was where he could get his mind together after a long day at work. But things weren't falling into place now.

He turned his attention back to Katie. ''So why are you telling me this? Why does this affect us?'' Not that there was really an *us*, he figured, but damn...

''Because there *is* a problem with the magic. Think of what this might mean for Mandy. I'm worried about what events I might put in motion if I make a gown for her. What if...well, what if?''

Jared froze for a moment, staring at Katie, then stifled a laugh as the tension drained out of him in a rush.

He really shouldn't make fun of Katie's—or her grandmother's—beliefs, especially when she seemed so troubled. But this was silly. He was afraid there might actually be an *issue.*

This could be cured in a sec. Then they could get back to where they left off, and he'd definitely invite her inside. They had plenty of time until Mandy came home, and he wanted to make the most of it.

Wanted to let her into his home and into his life.

"Jared? This isn't a joke."

"I know. And I'm worried about Mandy, too," he clarified. "But the kind of thread you might or might not use in her wedding gown—which I'm still hopeful she won't need, by the way—doesn't figure into it."

"I know it sounds insane." Exasperation tinged her voice. "But I can remember my grandmother telling me about this thread. Her exact words were, 'this thread is magic.' She was adamant that I treasure it and take care of it. She was practically on her death-bed when she gave it to me, so I know it was important to her—"

"No offense, Katie, but that doesn't mean—"

"It means something." Her tone was firm, sure. "I don't claim to know what the magic is or how it works, and it's that unknown part that I'm afraid of. I thought my grandmother was just babbling, so I didn't pay close enough attention. But look at the evidence! What if I make a dress for Mandy? Does that guarantee she'll marry Kevin? Does it guarantee a *happy* marriage, or will she be stuck in a marriage no matter what?"

Jared frowned at her in the darkness. "Katie, I told you. I can't imagine that an old spool of thread stuck to a pegboard in the back of your shop will make one bit of difference to what happens with Mandy. Not unless I use it to tie her bedroom door shut with her inside so she won't be able to run off with Kevin.''

"And I'm afraid it might.'' Agitation filled her voice. "I'm not sure I can live with that, knowing what I know. When I agreed to make a dress for her, I didn't believe my own reputation—not the way the *Gazette* portrayed it, at least. But now I'm not so sure. And if whatever this is between us continues…I don't know. But it's something we need to address. Don't you think?''

It was clear she took the whole crazy idea seriously. "Well, she's not married yet. So let's just assume that the thread—'' he nearly laughed just saying it ''—isn't going to make a difference. And if you're so worried it will, then just don't use it.''

Katie sat in silence, and he shifted to the side of the swing nearest her. "Katie—''

"I should get your tool belt before I forget.'' She pushed out of the chair, startling Scout, who hadn't anticipated she'd bolt from the rocker.

She took the front stairs with quick steps, and as she approached her Volkswagen, the motion light clicked on, illuminating the driveway. When she returned with the tool belt, he came to the stairs and took it from her with both hands.

"Look, Katie, I don't mean to make fun of your beliefs. Truly—''

"Hey, it's fine. I know you don't.''

Her smile was perfectly composed, as if the thirty-second jaunt to the car was enough for her to regain her equilibrium. "I told you, it wasn't something I believed in myself, not until I started digging deeper. And I still find it incredible. I can't expect you to just jump up and say, 'Of course, Katie! Of course you have magic thread!'"

But he could tell she did expect it. Despite her smile and her words, her eyes remained flat. He set the tool belt on the swing, then turned back to face her. "Is this why you feel we can't go forward with whatever it is that's happening between us? Because you feel you might somehow hurt my daughter—and me—by making her a dress?"

She nodded. "It's crazy. But that's a big part of it."

He waited, wondering what other part there could be, but she didn't say.

"Hey, it's late," she said, looking at her wristwatch. "Mandy's going to be home soon, and it's probably best if I'm not here."

"She won't be home for another hour."

"Better safe than sorry." Katie took a step backward, toward the stairs. She reached out to give Scout one last scratch between the ears, then eased down the stairs. "I'll see you tomorrow?"

He wrapped his fingers around the smooth wood of the porch railing and nodded. "I'll be able to finish my part of the job tomorrow. Then my countertop supplier will come to install that, and you'll be done. You'll have your shop all back to normal Friday afternoon, ready for customers."

"Great. Thanks again!"

She turned and walked to the car as if she thought Mandy would show up any second. Or as if she desperately needed to get away from him.

What was it? Something—something other than her harebrained magic-thread idea—bothered her. He'd assumed it was his background—his lack of higher education, the fact he'd never left Bowen—but he suspected that wasn't it at all.

He wondered if he'd ever find out. Or if they ever would get to Celestino's.

"All for the best, Porter," he grumbled to himself as he smiled and waved at Katie's Volkswagen while she turned it around, then spun the steering wheel to navigate the long driveway out to the road.

Turning to Scout and herding the German shepherd into the house, he said, "Whaddya think, old boy? Is this the universe's way of telling me I'm still not in a position to have a decent, normal relationship with a woman? That I'm bound to make a mess of things?"

He closed the front door behind them, then strode to the kitchen and grabbed the box of filters to start another pot of coffee.

Whether he was in a position to pursue a relationship or not, his heart was already heading down that road, and he wasn't sure he could stop it.

Chapter Eight

Katie punched the accelerator to the floor once she passed the final row of the Eberhardts' cornfields, leaving the dirt road to Jared's house behind her as she turned onto the highway.

Magic thread. She'd told him she believed in Oma's magic thread. So much for all the years she'd spent worrying about others' opinions and expectations.

"It's official, citizens of Bowen. I'm a loon," she muttered to herself as she sped past the dark alfalfa fields and toward the cluster of lights indicating that she was only a few miles from downtown Bowen. Heck, she was even talking to herself. No one in their right mind would believe in magic thread. Or at least no one in their right mind who *did* believe in it would actually voice that opinion aloud.

But as much as she tried to tell herself the entire concept was insane, she did believe it. Arguing about it with Jared made her realize the strength of her belief.

And the fact that Jared didn't believe—though she really couldn't expect any rational adult to buy into it—bothered her. Deeply. It smacked of her problems with Brett, and she had no desire to travel that path again. It had been painful enough the first time around to date a man, give him your heart and then find he didn't believe in you.

"Jared's perfectly normal," she told herself aloud. "He's not Brett."

Brett definitely wouldn't have believed in magic thread. Heck, Brett hadn't believed in *her* when she told him at graduation that she had no intention of getting a job in journalism. He'd thought she was foolish to pursue a career in design, making costumes for the stage in Boston. Even when she'd been working on *Miss Saigon* and *The Lion King,* getting to make some of the most elaborate costumes on stage, he'd made derogatory remarks, asking when she'd get a *real* job.

At first she'd chalked it up to Brett's big city corporate mentality. Working as an attorney at a large firm in downtown Boston certainly colored his views—not to mention that his father, a well-to-do investment banker, and his mother, a respected physician, ran in well-heeled circles. So she'd tried to prove herself, working harder at her job, getting him great seats, showing off her designs with pride. But in time, she'd wondered if the fact he viewed her career as nothing more than an interesting hobby indicated he would hesitate to support her in other areas. If he saw her as second class.

Good thing she'd never given him the opportunity to voice his opinion when the musical she'd been working on ended. She took the T home from the theater the week before the production closed, flopped onto the futon in her expensive, tiny South End apartment, and decided she missed life in Bowen—and that she'd rather go home and make wedding gowns than hunt for another job in theater design.

Oma would have been proud of her, both for honoring her family traditions and for being strong enough to make her own decisions and to leave any man who doubted her.

As she passed the city limit sign for Bowen, which was immediately followed by a sign indicating that the flowers along Main Street were courtesy of the Bowen Garden Club and Porter Construction, Katie whacked her hand against the wheel.

Maybe it was that Jared didn't believe in her—even if what she was asking of him was more than anyone could reasonably be expected to believe. But maybe it wasn't. After all, she couldn't see him trying to dissuade her from whatever path she might want to pursue in life. Unlike Brett, who seemed to think there were proper and not-so-proper jobs, Jared didn't seem the judgmental type.

So maybe it was fear for Mandy. And maybe it was fear that if Jared did believe in the magic, and Mandy did get married, he'd blame Katie for screwing up his daughter's life—after he'd spent years making sure Mandy wouldn't be trapped by her choices the way he had.

Then again, maybe it was just fear, period. She'd finally opened her mouth to say something unexpected, and look what happened.

She pulled into the narrow alley leading to the string of parking areas behind Main Street, then guided her car past the lot for Montfort's Deli and into her private parking space behind The Bowen Bride.

She loved living in the apartment above her shop. Loved the convenient access to work, the view of Main Street, the ease with which she could jog down the stairs, grab whatever she needed at the pharmacy or the grocery store, and be home again in less than ten minutes. Loved that it provided warm faces and friendly people during the day, even if, like Fred, they could be busybodies. Yet was a quiet, safe place to lay her head at night. She could call a friend anytime and walk to a café or to Montfort's to meet them. Her time was her own here.

Best of all, living right on Main Street afforded her enough of a town feel to remind her of Boston, but without all the noise and chaos. The worst it ever got was the day of the Fourth of July parade, and that was a fun kind of chaos. Plus she had a prime viewing spot from her second-floor windows.

Her life was damned good just as it was.

She closed her eyes for a moment and tried to clear her brain, then slipped her key into the lock at the back entrance. Maybe she was simply afraid that if she allowed a relationship with Jared to flourish, she would no longer be her own person. She'd be his girlfriend, or she'd be the focus of Mandy's desire for a mother figure.

And maybe, as had happened with Brett, she would feel compelled to try to live up to their expectations. She'd ruin the good life she'd built.

After locking the door behind her, she started up the stairs leading to her apartment. Halfway up she paused, took a deep breath, then turned and made her way back to her workshop and flipped on the light. On the far side of the table rested the two boxes with Oma's paperwork, while closer to her, the design books lay exactly as Mandy had arranged them earlier that afternoon.

After returning the boxes to the closet to make room on the table—and to keep them where she couldn't see them and think about the evidence they held—she flipped open the design book to the gown Mandy had selected, then went to her file cabinet to pull out the corresponding pattern.

Maybe the best way to get Jared and Mandy out of her mind was to make Mandy's wedding gown and be done with it. True, she'd told Mandy there was no rush, to wait a few months and see if she changed her mind, but it didn't matter anymore. If Mandy decided against the gown, she'd just suck up the cost of the materials. Playing with patterns and cutting fabric had always been her emotional therapy of preference. It beat consuming massive amounts of chocolate or ice cream, and tonight she needed some serious therapy.

And if things weren't going to work out with Jared…well then, she'd best get clear of the whole situation fast.

A sigh escaped her as she plunked her purse on a chair. No matter what her sense of self-preservation told her, she wanted things to work with Jared. It had taken every ounce of her will to break their kiss tonight, and she couldn't imagine never kissing him again.

As she strode through the workroom searching for the bolt of fabric she had in mind, her gaze fell upon the pegboard and the one spool of thread that looked so out of place. Even from several feet away, she could detect its frayed edges and the off-color hue that came with age. It certainly didn't look like golden thread spun by Sleeping Beauty on her enchanted spinning wheel.

Would it really make a difference to Mandy? She glanced toward the bolt of fabric she intended to use, then back to the thread. Jared had suggested she simply not use the thread, hadn't he?

She'd make that decision later. For now she would focus on the task at hand.

* * *

At the sound of jingling bells, Katie eased up on her machine's foot pedal. Now that her new counter was installed—thankfully, without having to spend more time alone with Jared, since a subcontractor installed the countertop—she'd booked three brides for fittings today.

She went through the motions of the first appointment on autopilot, shuffling the petite brunette into a curtained dressing area to try on her nearly-completed gown while the young woman yakked on about her plans to get married down in Omaha. Katie could barely follow who was from Bowen on the guest list of two hundred, or the bride's detailed plans for the reception at the Scoular Building ballroom.

Instead of engaging in the usual chatter, Katie kept quiet, only nodding and murmuring the occasional "Wow" or "How wonderful" as the bride bubbled over with excitement, giving her a full-blown description of the refurbished ballroom, as if Katie hadn't heard it from any other bride.

As she measured and pinned the hem on the gown, her mind remained firmly on Jared. And on the fact today was Friday.

The door jangled again, and Katie looked up expecting to see the next bride coming in, but instead she nearly swallowed a pin when Jared strode in wearing jeans, a black T-shirt bearing the Porter Construction logo, and heavy work boots.

Why did the man have to fill out his shirt so well?

And what was it about a man who knew how to wield a power tool?

"Hello, Liz. Beautiful gown," he commented to the bride-to-be.

"Thanks," she replied, beaming at the compliment, then looked down to where Katie crouched near her feet, holding the fabric at the bottom of the gown. "Mr. Porter built the most beautiful wall unit for my parents. They have a smokin' entertainment system now."

Katie couldn't stop the grin that came to her face. "He just finished building my cabinets."

"Noticed they were new since last time." She turned her face to Jared, careful to keep her body still as Katie finished pinning the hem of her gown. "They're very nice."

"Thank you." He stood silent for a moment, as if unsure whether to stay or go. Katie finally finished the gown, sent the bride back to the dressing room, then looked at Jared.

"I just wanted to see if you're still up for Celestino's," he said, keeping his voice low, though the bride could certainly overhear.

Katie couldn't possibly say no, not when he looked at her with those electric blue eyes, not when he stood right in front of her and she itched to reach out and smooth her fingers over his shirt, or to brush the stray fleck of sawdust off his cheek.

She wanted to go, but part of her still worried about

whether she and Jared would ever work if he didn't believe in her.

"Yeah, that's fine," she said before she could think about it any longer.

He frowned, and she expected him to say something like, *Don't get too excited about it,* but instead he said, "Seven okay? I have to run to Blair to look at a few potential jobs, so I won't be back in town until at least six or six-thirty."

"Seven's great," she replied, hoping she sounded more enthusiastic. He nodded, then turned on the heel of his boot and left.

"That man is freaking gorgeous," the bride-to-be commented as she exited the dressing room, her gown folded carefully over one arm. Katie took the gown and arranged it on a hanger.

"If I wasn't marrying Rick..." Liz raised an eyebrow and cocked her head toward the door. Just beyond, Jared was climbing into his blue pickup. "Of course, he's too old for me. He probably couldn't keep up with me, if you know what I mean."

Katie smiled, though suddenly she wanted to smack the girl. Jared definitely wasn't old. And if this girl knew how the man could...well, she'd have no doubts about his ability to keep up with anyone.

"I'll have your gown finished next week," Katie said, trying to shake the thought of Jared's slow, long kisses. "Is there a day you can come in to pick it up?"

She hardly heard the brunette's babbling as she

griped about her busy schedule—going into Omaha for a cake tasting, getting invitations to the calligrapher, arranging for party favors to be delivered to the reception site. Katie just hoped Mandy wouldn't be making arrangements like those anytime soon. Or that Jared wouldn't hate her if she did.

Okay, it wasn't as if he was used to dating and knowledgeable about these things. But the silence filling the cab of his truck as they followed Highway 75 toward the tiny town of Herman couldn't be normal.

Witty banter. He needed to engage her in witty banter.

"So, any idea what you want to order? Know what their specialty is?"

"No, not really."

So much for wit.

They passed the city limit sign for Herman and he slowed the truck to a crawl. "Bet Harry's hanging out behind the mill with his radar detector."

"I'll take that bet. I've never seen him here during the dinner hour. I think he'd rather eat than earn money for the good citizens of Herman."

"All three hundred or so of them." Jared grinned, then turned to look into the driveway on the side of the mill as they passed. "You lose. He's there."

"Deli bag on the dash, though. Told you he wouldn't miss dinner."

"What else is there to do in Herman?"

"Not much," she admitted. "But I can already

smell Celestino's. I can't believe they're going to make a go of it here.''

He looked down one of the side streets of the nearly empty town. ''Well, they're certainly pulling in people from Bowen. And one of the roofing guys at Porter Construction said he and his wife drove over from Craig last week to try it. Said half the town was there. But you're right. It's tough to make a go of a small business around here. Though you've done well with yours.''

''So far,'' she acknowledged as he turned the truck onto Fifth Street, heading toward West Street and Celestino's. ''But what about you? That day in my shop, you said—''

''Oh, no.'' He wanted nothing more than to talk to Katie about his plans, to see how she really felt about his desire to open his own business, but the sight in the parking lot at the corner of Fifth and West took precedence.

''Is that Kevin Durban's car?'' Katie asked.

''Yep. And they don't look like they're having dinner.''

Katie started to ask what he meant, but stopped when saw the young couple. Mandy and Kevin were standing in the Celestino's parking lot, their position at the front of Kevin's Pontiac keeping them partially obscured from the road.

''Did you know they'd be here?''

Jared shook his head, then pulled over to the side of the street. ''And I didn't tell her about our plans, just that I'd be out and that she had to be home by ten and take her cell phone with her.''

''They don't look too happy.''

Jared agreed with Katie's assessment. Kevin had his baseball hat pulled down low, and his hands were jammed into the pockets of his baggy jeans. Mandy stood facing him, arms crossed, hugging herself. Though he couldn't see her face very well now that the sun was dipping below the horizon, he knew something major was taking place.

''Maybe we shouldn't,'' Katie said. ''Let's give them some privacy.''

''Shame to miss out on that meal,'' Jared said. The mixed smells of fresh garlic and tomato sauce drifted on the air, making his stomach rumble in response. He rarely ate this late. In his line of work, he often arrived on a job site by 7:00 a.m. and left by four-thirty, so he could make dinner for Mandy by five. ''But I agree. So where to?''

''Not much choice unless we drive on to Blair, but you might want to be home for Katie later, in case she needs you.''

''Montfort's, then? I'm not sure what else to do.'' He turned the truck, then drove around the block until they were back at Highway 75. A left took them back to Bowen, a right toward Blair.

They looked at each other across the space of the front seat. People would talk if they showed up at Montfort's together on a Friday night and they both knew it. Though judging from the crowded parking lot at Celestino's, people might have seen them here just as easily.

"Montfort's is fine, unless you're a secret gourmet."

"You'd have to ignore the coffee grounds in my sink. And be willing to eat mac and cheese."

He turned the truck toward Bowen, then hazarded a glance her way after they passed Harry, who waved to them as they passed his police cruiser, which was still hidden behind the mill to catch speeders entering town. When Katie smiled at the sight of the officer, he decided that yes, he could do this. He could have a woman in his home and make her dinner.

But not tonight.

"I really can cook. I'm no gourmet, but I make a mean pan of stuffed manicotti. I'm afraid I haven't been to the grocery store lately, though. I was planning to go in the morning."

"In that case, let's go to Montfort's. If it looks crowded—or if the Fred Winston gossip types are there—we can always go to my shop to eat our sandwiches if we want. I happen to know there's a brand new counter installed, so all that mess is out of the main room and the table's back where it belongs, ready for diners."

"Sounds like a plan."

He pushed harder on the accelerator as they cleared Herman city limits. As much as he wanted dinner, his mind remained split between Katie—and whether or not this date would improve things between them—and his daughter.

Mandy and Kevin fighting was a good thing, he supposed, if it meant she'd reconsider marriage. But he didn't want her hurt, either. And Kevin was a perfectly good kid, and good for Mandy.

"Can't stop thinking about her, can you?"

"Number-one requirement in the dad job description."

"For good dads." She leaned forward and ran a finger over his dash. "I was wondering. How old's this truck, anyway?"

"Celebrated it's thirteenth this year."

"And you've kept it in pretty good shape. For the kind of beating it must take, carting around wood and tools, it looks pretty good."

"Rusting out in one wheel well, though."

"But you haven't bought a new one. Saving your pennies?"

Ah. Now they were getting into it again—the conversation she'd started just before he spotted Mandy and Kevin. "Yep."

"And that's why you're such a good dad. It's hard to put a kid through college, especially starting out where you did, right out of high school. I wasn't nearly as mature when I graduated college. I didn't even think about things like buying a house or saving for any children I might have."

"Well," he admitted, "I had to be mature, since I already had the child. But that's not the only reason

I've been careful and saving up." He took a deep breath, wondering if she'd react as he hoped, or as he told himself to expect. "You know I want to start my own business. Well, I'm almost ready to do it."

"I told you before, I think you'd be great. What, exactly, would you do, though? You said you'd never directly compete with Stewart."

She seemed genuinely curious, but he had to know why. Did it matter to her? "I've always wanted to make furniture. I love the woodworking I do in people's homes—the built-in shelves, the fireplace mantels, that kind of thing—but I would love to make high-quality furniture. Solid tables, dressers, beds. Furniture that can be handed down from generation to generation. Something that allows for experimentation, for real craftsmanship."

"Wow."

"What can I say? I'm a furniture geek."

"Never heard of anyone being a furniture geek, but I'll take your word for it," she said, grinning.

"I'm hoping to rent some space on Main Street, maybe a block off, if I have to, and open a small showroom. But it's a risk. Kind of like opening an Italian restaurant in a town of three hundred. The odds are against success. And since I'd be doing everything custom, it'll take a while to really get things going."

"I'm quite familiar with the perils, believe me, though my shop already had a good reputation, thanks to my grandmother. You'll be facing a real challenge."

He slowed down, avoiding a squirrel who had the audacity to run onto the road despite the decreasing visibility. Once he hit cruising speed again, Jared asked, "Does it make a difference to you? If I succeed, I mean?"

Katie turned toward him, and he could feel her frown, despite being unable to turn and see her expression in the now-dark cab. "Of course I want you to do well. What would make you say that?"

"Well, when we talked on the porch the other night, you said that the thread and Mandy were only part of what made you cautious." He flicked his gaze toward her for a moment before turning his focus back to the road. "There was another part, wasn't there?"

"I don't understand."

"Reputation means a lot around here, when you see the same people year in and year out. You knew something about me before I ever stepped in your shop. You knew about my daughter from Fred. You knew Stewart's reputation, and that I worked for him. And I knew something about you from Stewart. It's the way things work in a small town. It's part of why you're successful in your business."

He slowed the truck again as they entered Bowen, though he knew there wouldn't be any speed traps at this time of night. A group of high-schoolers gathered near the gas station, leaning against their cars and talking, probably deciding whether or not to drive out of town to catch the latest Julia Roberts or Nicole Kidman flick.

He remembered when he'd been one of them, hanging out on the corner with Corey and a group of their friends, talking about the weekend's Railroader football game or whether their parents would let them stay out late enough to go bowling in Blair. In many ways he felt as if it'd just been a few weeks or months ago, but when he thought of Mandy, it seemed a lifetime.

"What I need to know," he said as he spun the truck into one of the Main Street parking spaces near Montfort's, "is if you need to date a certain sort of person. If reputation matters."

She turned toward him, though her seat belt stayed on. "I'd have a difficult time dating a felon, if that's what you mean. You have a secret I need to know?"

He shook his head. "You think anyone could keep a secret like that here? Believe me, there's no prison record. Amazing, since I'm sure Corey's parents would have thrown me in jail if they'd had the where-withal."

He drummed his fingers against the steering wheel. "But they aren't the only ones in town who've always thought the worst of me. Look at Fred. He doesn't intend to look down on me, but he does, and he's one of the nicest guys around."

"Fred doesn't mean anything by his comments. Don't take what he says personally. I'm sure he's said a thing or two about me over the years, too."

He let go of the steering wheel and turned to Katie, making certain she understood. "It's not the same. You should see the stares I sometimes get when I come to church with Mandy. Even now, all these years later, people sometimes whisper and point out the guy who knocked up sweet little Cornelia Welsh and upset her so much she had to move. And who knows what he did afterward, because Corey's poor parents ended up moving, too."

"Jared—"

"They say that Stewart was a dear to hire me and give me a means to support Mandy. They even wonder—sometimes aloud, intending for me to hear—how a man like me could possibly raise a girl all alone."

"I don't think those things, Jared." She put a hand out and tentatively touched the back of his hand. He wanted nothing more than to grab it and kiss it—to kiss her everywhere—but he had to know.

"Is the reason you want me to be a success—the reason you constantly compliment me on my parenting—because you want to make sure my reputation is good enough for you?" He flipped over his hand, capturing hers within. "If you feel that way, believe me, I won't think less of you. I actually understand. I've always felt it was fine to have those kind of judgments in your heart when it came to friends or other people about town. To just believe what your gut tells you and go with it. But if we go further, I need more.

Things are different when you're looking at a potential husband or wife. The standards are higher.''

''I agree. And believe me, I do know how people here talk. I've always been more concerned with my own reputation than I should be, simply because of who my grandparents were.''

He took a deep breath and squeezed her fingers briefly before letting go of her hand. ''I need to know that you'd want to date me even if I never open my own shop, or if I go belly up in a year and have to go back to working for Stewart. That, in your deepest heart, you don't care that I don't have a fancy education like you do and probably never will. I need to know you won't care that people will whisper about you the minute they believe you're seeing me. Otherwise, there's not much point in going forward.''

''People think more highly of you than you believe, Jared.''

She meant to make him feel better, and he loved that about her. Katie was going to make a wonderful mom someday, and she'd make someone a wonderful wife. He just didn't know if he was the man for her. If, in her heart, she could really make that leap from saying all the right things to feeling all the right things.

''You don't know until you've walked in my shoes.'' His voice sounded rough, even to his own ears, but he had to be certain. ''Katie, I don't want our relationship to be contingent on my success. Mandy is the only person who's ever truly believed in me one hundred percent. There's a connection between you and me I can't even begin to explain, so if you're having doubts, I need to know that now. Not a month or six months from now. Or when my business fails to take off. Or when people like Fred, who mean well but are completely clueless, start warning you away from me.''

Katie crossed her arms over her chest and leaned back so her head rested against the glass of the window. ''That's all you want from me? That I believe in you?''

''I'm not asking you to. I want you clear on that point. I've always felt that a person can't force anyone to believe something. I'm simply asking whether or not you do.''

Chapter Nine

"Jared, I can't say."

"I see." Jared turned away from her and stared straight ahead. Kate followed his line of sight, looking through the spotless windshield toward the windows lining the front of Montfort's. Now that darkness had fallen, it was easy to observe a group of teens dropping their tips on a table and leaving. Two families occupied a pair of booths along the windows, and further inside, Gloria stood near a table with a plastic bin, filling it with dirty glassware.

"It's not what you think," Katie replied.

She reached out and put her hand on his knee. Doing so was dangerous to her psyche, but somehow her urge to comfort him overrode her own desire for self-protection. Did the guy not have a clue? "Look, let's eat. I'm dying of hunger here. The dinner hour is pretty much past, and no one we know is in there—well, other than the Montforts—if you're worried about being seen together, which I am definitely not.''

She gave his knee a quick, light pat, then hopped out of the truck and shut the door, getting to the curb before Jared even got his own door open.

''I'd have opened your door for you, you know,'' he mumbled, which made Katie smile inside. Of course he would have.

''I might have a certain reputation, but that doesn't mean I'm impolite.''

''Jared? Get over it already.''

He stopped short outside the door to Montfort's. ''Come again?''

''I said get over it. Yes, people in town might think of you a certain way, but not the people who've spent time with you, and not me.'' She gave him a slow smile, hoping to put his mind at ease. ''So get over it.''

When he stared at her in silence, she gestured toward the door. ''I'll let you open that one.''

He stepped past her and grabbed the heavy bar to pull open the glass door, then gestured for her to enter ahead of him. Gloria waved them in, calling out from behind the counter that they were free to take any table and she'd bring out two of her brand-new menus.

''Gotta love sit-down service at night. Sure beats the long line at lunch,'' Katie commented.

Clearly, though, Jared's mind remained fixed on

something besides fresh sandwiches and soup. "Wait a minute. What did you mean by—"

"Look." Katie paused to take a menu from Gloria, making sure to pay her a compliment on the new design before the restaurant owner hustled to grab a booster seat for a grumpy toddler. "You're assuming that your past is the reason I can't answer you. Did you ever consider that it might be mine?"

Jared picked up his menu, but didn't open it. His determined blue eyes locked her in place. "It's because I questioned you about the thread, isn't it? Look, I've been thinking about that a lot, and I wanted to say—"

She smiled at him over the top of her menu and shook her head. How could a man be so devastatingly handsome, so magnetic, yet so normal at the same time?

And how could it have taken her this long to realize that Jared was a living, breathing example of everything she should have been doing her entire life—living the way he knew was best, rather than trying to either live up to or escape the expectations of others?

"No, please don't apologize. It's not so much the fact you questioned me about the thread as it is the reason I reacted as I did and bolted out of there." A light laugh escaped her. "You know, it's a good thing Harry works for the Herman police force instead of Bowen's, 'cause I'd have gotten a ticket for sure coming back into town from your place. Think I spun gravel into the Eberhardts' fields as it is.''

"So why did you? Bolt, I mean.''

"I was afraid you wouldn't believe in *me*. When you laughed at the thread, I wondered what else you might find funny, what else you might not take seriously about me, you know?''

Jared leaned forward. "What do you mean? Like what?''

"Like the fact I'm in my thirties and single, which is practically a crime in this town. Like the fact I left, had a successful career, then came back again—''

"Why did you come back? I can't imagine it was because you were dying to live in the middle of nowhere. Your life in Boston had to be exciting. All the plays you were working on, all the great people and things to do.''

The toddler sitting near the window with his parents threw his sippy cup on the floor, and it rolled toward Katie. She scooped the cup up and handed it to the mother, who headed out the door saying something about it being past her son's bedtime while the father hurriedly paid Gloria and packed up their food in doggie bags.

"But that's just it,'' Katie said once the ruckus died down. "I missed Bowen. It's a cliché to say that city people aren't as friendly as those in the rural Midwest, and that everyone here is pure hearted while everyone there is inconsiderate. Life isn't as cut and dried as that. But I did miss being here—there's a different world view you have when you grow up someplace like Bowen, when your whole family lives within a twenty-mile radius and has for generations. When your family helped found the town. As much as I loved working in the theater, I realized that Boston wasn't what I'd hoped for. I felt adrift.''

''What had you hoped for?''

''Mostly I wanted to stop feeling trapped. You know how hard it was growing up in Bowen, being my grandparents' only grandchild? How hard it is to live up to expectations? I can't tell you how many times my grandmother, and then my father, told me I'd grow up to marry, in their words, 'a good Nebraska man, and settle down.' When they told me that at seventeen, I was certain it was a death sentence. I wanted a career. I wanted adventure. And the thought of marrying some boring guy from Bowen and spending the rest of my life here just chilled me.''

Jared's mouth curved up on one side, showing he found the humor in her statement, given their current situation—not to mention what had happened to him with Corey. ''So you ran.''

''So I ran.'' She reached across the table and, ignoring Gloria and Evelyn Montfort's curious glances from behind the deli counter, she squeezed Jared's hand. ''I do understand Corey and her urge to run. Living in a town where your every move is under a microscope, especially when she was in a situation she couldn't handle, had to be difficult.''

Jared looked down at her hand in his, then raised

his blue eyes up to meet hers. "Bowen made you feel trapped."

"Yes. But when I got to Boston, I realized that a person can feel trapped anywhere. Expectations aren't limited to people who live in small towns." Before she knew it, she was pouring her heart out to Jared about Brett. About how he wanted her to be someone she wasn't, about how he didn't believe in her.

She paused for a minute while Evelyn came out to take their order. After handing over the menus to the inquisitive restaurant owner, she smiled at Jared, who still seemed unsure about drawing the attention of the Montfort sisters.

"In the end, I came back to Bowen because I love it here. All the things that I hated when I was a teenager made me crave this town ten years later. I wanted to take a chance on making a living doing what my grandmother did, even when all the small towns around us are shrinking even further, even when chain stores can sell a wedding gown for a half to a third of what I can, even though life here isn't as glamorous as working on a big theater production."

She exhaled, then shifted her napkin to her lap. Meeting Jared's gaze again, she said, "So that's why I get it. The whole thing with your brother, the whole thing with Corey, even."

"I should have known," Jared acknowledged. "But you have to see why I had to question it. You've had all those experiences I've never had—life in Boston, of all places—and you have a fabulous education I'm sure I'll never get at this point in my life."

"All the things Corey left you for." The words came out in a near whisper, but Jared heard every syllable.

"Exactly. Not that I don't think I'm intelligent, of course," he pointed out with a grin. "I've worked my tail off, built a wonderful home, and I'm excited about opening a business soon. I also have a hell of a daughter. I would like to think I had something to do with the way she's turned out. But that doesn't completely erase the past. Or up the chance I'll be successful in the future. I need to know that you believe anyway."

Katie felt tears well up in her eyes, but she managed to blink them back. How many years had Jared been made to feel less than the man he truly was, simply because he'd made one mistake back in high school? A mistake that wasn't his alone, and that happened to thousands of teens every year?

She took a deep breath. "Jared, I could never *not* believe in you, or in the fact you're pursuing what you want to do in life. Education and time living in a big city don't mean that I don't have the exact same dreams and insecurities as you do. In fact, listening to you in the truck tonight, I learned one hell of a lesson. I need to stop worrying about what everyone else around me is thinking. I need to live like you do."

He started to say something but stopped.

"Jared, sometimes you just have to believe for the sake of believing. And I do believe in you."

Under the table, Jared's foot hooked her chair. Slowly he pulled it as close to the table as possible. "I'm sorry I laughed at the thread."

"It's okay—"

"And I'm sorry about Brett, too. He was a fool not to realize what he had in you. You were right to leave him."

"I know."

"Because I know a good Nebraska man who does realize what a treasure you are. One who has no expectations other than the hope that you'd believe in him, and one who'd go out of his way to ensure you never feel trapped."

His voice dropped to a whisper as Gloria approached. "Because I'm falling in love with you just the way you are, and I wouldn't want to ruin that."

Gloria walked past them with a rag in hand to wash up one of the nearby tables. Both Jared and Katie tried to hide their grins when they noticed how slowly she swirled the cloth over the tabletop, obvious in her attempt to overhear as much of their conversation as possible.

Katie tried to ignore the older woman, though her heart was doing a slow flip-flop. Jared was falling in love with her?

"Hey, Gloria," Jared said when the older woman started cleaning the table a second time. "How long on the subs?"

Gloria stiffened but plastered an innocent smile across her face. "Oh, just another minute. Evelyn's got them just about finished."

"Great." Jared winked at Katie, then added, "And, Gloria, can we get them to go?"

"Of course." Gloria pretended to work at a stubborn spot on the tabletop, then walked past Jared and Katie. Just as she reached the counter and glanced back at them, Jared leaned across the table, slid his hand around to the back of Katie's head, and pulled her forward for a kiss.

Katie smiled against his warm mouth, feeling like a giddy schoolgirl making out behind the high school, knowing that the teachers were probably watching.

"Thank you," Jared said against her mouth, then kissed her again, despite the low gasp Katie guessed came from Evelyn.

"For what?" Katie asked as he released her.

"For falling in love with me, too. Just the way I am. No one's ever done that before, and it feels," he couldn't help but grin as he said it, "magic."

Ten minutes later, Katie jammed her keys into the front door of The Bowen Bride, then pushed through the glass door with Jared at her heels. She flipped the light switch next to the front door so they wouldn't bump into the table, then pulled him back, toward her workroom. "Remember when we ate subs here on your birthday? You asked me if it was a pity date."

"It was pretty pitiful."

"Yeah, well I can tell you that it absolutely is *not* a pity date tonight."

"Good."

As they passed the round table where she usually had brides page through her design books, the Montfort's bag hit it with a thump.

Katie laughed aloud. "So much for the subs."

"And good thing we didn't order soup," Jared teased.

Katie meant to take Jared through the back, up to her apartment, but his hand tightened around hers, and he tugged, pulling her back against his chest just as they crossed the threshold of the workroom. Katie turned her head just in time to see him flick the curtain off its hook so it fell closed.

Instantly his arms wrapped around her and his mouth found hers. It had been one thing to kiss him in her workroom in the middle of the day. A little daring, a little flirty. And when he'd kissed her on his front porch, with the motion light from the driveway beaming at her back, she'd been so filled with concern about the thread—and guilt about what it meant for Mandy—that she couldn't think straight.

But this—kissing in the darkness of the back room, with the only light the faint red glow of the Exit sign leading to the back door—set every bit of her screaming with want, and provided the heady sensation of knowing she'd get exactly what she wanted.

And that Jared wanted it, too.

She wrapped her arms around Jared's broad back,

pulling his body as close to hers as possible. Even his back, Katie discovered, was rock solid from years of work, both as a carpenter and around the house, spending his weekends on tasks like building the shed she saw standing alongside his house or the treehouse she knew he'd built in the backyard for Mandy when she was a girl.

"You feel incredible," Jared murmured as he moved to kiss her cheek, then her neck. His warm breath against her skin sent Katie into a spell of dizziness, and she let her hands slide down Jared's back toward his waist and below. Could the man have a more perfect body?

"So you think I'm falling in love with you?" she whispered against his lips as she allowed her fingers to explore the back of his waistband. She pulled his shirt free and ran her hands along his firm, warm skin. Jared's mouth returned to hers, and a low moan sounded at the back of his throat as he kissed her harder. His cheek brushed hers, and she found herself wishing she could wake up with that cheek on the pillow beside hers. She could imagine reaching over in the morning, running her fingers across that skin to wake him, teasing him about the light stubble she knew would be there. Then making love to him before sharing breakfast and talking about their dreams and ambitions.

"Yes, ma'am. I'm pretty certain of it." His hand came up to cup her breast through her shirt just as she wrapped one leg around the back of his. Katie swayed for a moment at the sensation of his fingers and their slow, loving massage. Then she started imagining what else they might be capable of, and a moan slipped out at the mental picture.

They couldn't get any closer with their clothes still on, and Katie had a feeling he didn't want to stop any more than she did.

"The door to my apartment's right there," she breathed close to his ear as he moved to kiss her neck. "Might be more comfortable."

"Well, it is a little odd to be kissing a woman in a room full of wedding gowns," Jared laughed against her throat as he lifted her just enough to take a few awkward steps toward the apartment door, carrying her in front of him. "Not that I mind the kissing. But it's a good thing none of these gowns are for Mandy. Now that would be really weird."

"Actually," Katie hesitated, then pulled back from Jared, just far enough to see his face in the dim light. "I did start her gown. I probably shouldn't have—I didn't need to yet—but I did."

"Oh." She couldn't see well enough to tell if he was angry, or confused, or what, but he didn't step out of her embrace, and she had to take that as a good sign. She couldn't imagine how empty she'd feel if he let go of her now.

"But I didn't use the thread," she explained. "It's the very last thing I do. I stitch it into the hem. And...I know you don't believe in the magic or my Oma's stories. And I still don't expect you to. But I want you to know that I wouldn't have put it in her hem until I talked to you again. I just felt strange about it. It's always been second nature—just something I do when I finish a gown—but this time it felt wrong.''

"Maybe because it is wrong." Jared ran a finger over her lips gently to stop her protest. "Not that you're wrong about the thread or its magic. It's the marriage that's probably wrong."

When she nodded, he added, "I can't say I believe one hundred percent in magic thread. But after we talked on the porch, I did start to wonder. And now if things between Mandy and Kevin are strained, maybe…I don't know.''

"Maybe they were never meant to be married. Or maybe the thread doesn't matter until it's actually in a gown. I wish I knew."

He nodded, then leaned forward and dropped his forehead against hers. "Have you ever had a bride come into the shop, order a gown, then change her mind?"

"Never. Though we don't know for certain Mandy's changed her mind."

"Not yet, but after what we saw tonight, I have a gut feeling." Jared raised his head just enough to look in the direction of the spool of thread, though Katie knew he couldn't possibly pick it out in the darkness. "It does seem like an awful lot of coincidences, though. All those couples still married."

"I'll get you to believe yet," she teased, then

spread her fingers across the sides his face, pulling his mouth closer to hers. "You're not angry that I started on her gown?"

"No. Definitely not angry." She could feel the rise of his cheeks under her fingertips as he smiled, and their lips connected again without either of them missing a beat. "In fact, I don't think I've been this happy in a long, long time."

"Neither have I." They shared another kiss, deeper and filled with promise. She was just about to pull him toward the door leading to her upstairs apartment as the tinkle of bells sounded at the front door.

"Did you leave it unlocked?" Jared asked in a whisper.

"Umm." She reluctantly pulled back and added, "Suppose I was in a bit of a hurry."

"We're making a bad habit of this."

She reached out a hand to lift the curtain just as a tentative voice asked, "Dad? Are you here?"

Jared planted a quick kiss on top of Katie's head, a promise that they'd pick up where they left off as soon as he finished with his daughter, then strode through the curtain. "Mandy? What are you doing here?"

Mandy's gaze flicked from her father to Katie, and Katie noticed the teen intentionally keeping her eyes averted from her father's half-untucked shirt. Then Mandy glimpsed the Montfort's bag abandoned on the front table, and her eyes widened.

"I'm sorry, I hope I'm not interrupting—are you two, um, like, on a date? I'm so sorry to bother—"

"Mandy, you know you're never, ever a bother," Katie assured her.

Jared nodded his agreement. "So what's going on?"

Mandy crossed her arms over her chest. "I was, um, out with Kevin, and I saw your truck at Montfort's, so I had him drop me off. I didn't want to be home alone. When you weren't in the restaurant, Evelyn told me she thought you and Katie'd come over here." She swallowed hard. "I'm really sorry to interrupt."

Jared walked to the front of the store and put a hand on his daughter's shoulder. "What happened?"

"It's Kevin." She choked on his name. Jared pulled her toward the small table so she could sit, then took the seat across from her and told her to start at the beginning.

Katie started to excuse herself so Mandy and Jared could talk privately, but Mandy shook her head. "It's okay, Katie. I need to talk to you, too. Would you stay?"

Katie glanced at Jared. He didn't seem bothered, so she went to stand behind him. "Did you and Kevin break up?"

She shook her head. "No. But we're not getting married. Not now." She met her father's frown and said, "I know you're going to say you told me so—"

"I won't."

Mandy sniffed. "Well, I told Kev that I called my mother."

"You didn't tell me that."

"I know, Dad. And I'm really sorry. I just—I don't know what I was thinking. But she never called me back, anyway. When I told Kev about it, he got all weird."

"Did he say why?"

"He said we really should think more about whether to go ahead with the wedding, and that maybe my mother not calling me is a sign."

She grabbed a tissue from a box Katie held out to her, then looked at her dad. "Kev said he loves me and all that stuff, but he was looking at everything we have to do when we start school. And he's kind of freaked. He's worried I'm going to meet someone who's all into astronomy, since that's what I want to major in, and said it would make sense, because even if we were married and living together, he'd hardly ever see me. I'd be clear across campus from where his classes are all day long. We're both going to be around completely different people since he wants to major in agribusiness, and he thought we should see if we can make it through college together before we get married. That if we do, then we'll know it's for real."

Jared sighed and grabbed one of Mandy's hands. "What do you think, sweetheart? You disagree?"

A lone tear ran down Mandy's face and dropped onto the table. She swiped it with her free hand, then looked at her dad. "No. I think he's right. But I don't want him to be right. I don't want to lose him."

She glanced up at Katie. "What do you think? You're so smart about this stuff."

"Me?" Katie couldn't hide her look of shock. "Trust me, I don't know anything."

"You know plenty," Jared assured her over his shoulder. Turning back to Mandy, he said, "You need to do what your heart and your gut tell you to do. I think Katie would agree with me on that. If you love Kevin and he loves you, sometimes you just have to believe."

Mandy nodded, then stood and rounded the table to hug her father. "Thanks, Dad."

For a few minutes he simply held her, letting her sniffle against his shirt. When she finally pulled away, she was smiling. "And thanks for not saying you told me so. And for not being too mad at me."

"I'm always here for you. You know that. But we'll have to talk about Corey later. And how calling her might not have been the smartest move."

"I know." She gave Katie a hug and added, "And thank you, too. You hardly knew me and you've been so, so nice to me. Thanks."

Katie smiled. "It was nothing. I'm glad we've gotten to know each other."

Mandy glanced toward the workroom, and a look of discomfort flitted across her face. "You haven't started the gown yet, have you?"

"I started, but I didn't get very far."

"So what's your policy on—"

"Don't worry about the gown, Mandy."

"I'll pay for it," Jared interrupted them. "You can always come back here in a few years and have it finished, or you can have Katie finish it now and put it away for later. Whatever works. Sound like a plan?"

He looked from Mandy to Katie, then back to Mandy.

"I'm not sure, Dad. I mean, I love the design I picked out and everything, but it feels wrong now."

Katie put an arm around Mandy's shoulder. "Understandable. I'll take care of it. Don't worry about it anymore."

"Okay," Mandy said. "It's such a pretty design, though. Maybe you can find a good use for it. I mean, if you ever decide to get married, I bet it'd fit you. You're maybe a couple inches taller than me, but we're the same size. Since I'm assuming you haven't hemmed it yet…well, I'm just saying that if you want to make it so it fits you, just for someday, that'd be cool."

"Thanks, Mandy," Katie gave the teen a warm hug. "I don't anticipate getting married anytime soon—"

"But never say never, right?" Jared leaned against the counter, his arms crossed over his chest, and shot her a lazy, wicked smile.

"I did interrupt something, didn't I?" Mandy asked. "Ohmigosh. I did. Dad!"

"I should probably take you home, young lady, before your imagination gets the better of you," Jared teased. "But how about if we invite Katie over for dinner? I happen to know she hasn't eaten yet."

Before Katie could protest, Mandy clapped her hands. "That would rock! And I promise to leave you alone after dinner."

"That's not—"

"Dad, just deal."

Mandy glanced at the Montfort's bag, which was still on the front table where Jared had dropped it when he and Katie came in. "Did you happen to get a veggie sub for me, though? Kevin and I never got around to eating tonight."

"We can run back into Montfort's before we leave."

Mandy beamed, and Katie couldn't help but admire her. Despite her heartbreak, she was excited for her father, and accepting of her. "I'd love that. Katie? Please come over."

"Hmm. You have any good movies? Any popcorn?"

"Yes to both, but that's not a very exciting way to spend the evening," Jared answered. A slow smile spread across his face as he added, "Sitting in a house in the middle of nowhere, watching a movie you've probably already seen with a boring old Nebraska carpenter and his just-dumped teenage daughter."

"Hey, I wasn't dumped!"

"And you are neither old nor boring," Katie

added. She strode to the front door and opened it, waving Jared and Mandy out ahead of her. "On the contrary, I think it'll be the most exciting evening I've had in a long time."

As Jared passed her, he leaned in and whispered, "And I've been wanting to have a wonderful woman like you over for dinner for a long time, too."

Epilogue

Jared couldn't remember the last time he felt the urge to cry. Maybe the day after Mandy was born, when he held her in the hospital, overwhelmed with the knowledge he was her father and responsible for her. Panicked, and yet so full of love and hope at the same time.

But as the first strains of the wedding march echoed through the church, he knew today topped it.

"Are you ready? It's your turn to walk." He grinned at the beautiful young woman who looped her arm though his. He could hardly believe it'd only been six years since he'd watched from the other end of the aisle as Katie made this walk, wearing a heart-stopping, elegant white wedding gown. And now he would escort Mandy down the same aisle as she wore the same gown.

No, now that he thought about it, he had very

nearly cried at his own wedding, watching as Mandy had taken Katie's bouquet and stood behind Katie as her maid of honor. He'd held his wife-to-be's hands and listened to her promise to love him for the rest of her days. He'd never been as happy or as at peace as he'd been at that very moment.

"Mom looks so excited," Mandy said, nodding toward Katie, who rose as Mandy and Jared came to stand at the back of the church, their toes just touching the aisle runner. "She really does love you, Dad."

As the rest of the wedding guests followed Katie's lead and stood, and the organist began to play the wedding march, Jared placed a hand over Mandy's and smiled at his daughter. "No, sweetie. She loves us."

"You know, I never thought I'd have my mother at my wedding. But I really feel I do, that Katie's my mother in every way. Guess I'm pretty lucky."

"We both are."

As he walked her down the aisle, instead of taking in the sight of her flowers, the guests, or her nervous but thrilled groom, she turned to him and said, "Dad, I hope I remember this forever. I can't believe it. It just feels…magical."

As they reached the front of the church, just before he gave away Mandy to her giddy groom and went to sit with his gorgeous wife, he leaned over and whispered in her ear, taking pains that no one else in the church could hear.

"Believe in the magic, Mandy. It's real. I know."

*   *   *   *   *

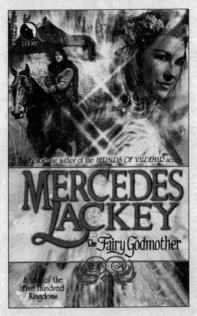

If you enjoyed what you just read,
then we've got an offer you can't resist!

Take 2 bestselling
love stories FREE!

Plus get a FREE surprise gift!

SILHOUETTE *Romance*®

In a
Fairy Tale
World

Six reluctant couples.
Five classic love stories.
One matchmaking princess.
And time is running out!

Don't miss a moment of this enchanting miniseries from Silhouette Romance.

Their Little Cowgirl by MYRNA MACKENZIE
Silhouette Romance #1738

Rich Man, Poor Bride by LINDA GOODNIGHT
Silhouette Romance #1742
Available November 2004

Her Frog Prince by SHIRLEY JUMP
Silhouette Romance #1746
Available December 2004

Engaged to the Sheik by SUE SWIFT
Silhouette Romance #1750
Available January 2005

Nighttime Sweethearts by CARA COLTER
Silhouette Romance #1754
Available February 2005

Twice a Princess by SUSAN MEIER
Silhouette Romance #1758
Available March 2005

Only from Silhouette Books!

Coming in December 2004

SILHOUETTE *Romance* ®

presents a brand-new book from

Roxann Delaney

Look for...

THE TRUTH ABOUT PLAIN JANE, #1748

She'd come to the Triple B Dude Ranch for the chance to
make her mark in the world of reporting. But going
undercover becomes a risky proposition when
Meg Chastain finds the most tempting story is
her feelings for confirmed bachelor and
ranch owner Trey Brannigan.

Available at your favorite retail outlet.

SILHOUETTE *Romance*

COMING NEXT MONTH

#1746 HER FROG PRINCE—Shirley Jump
In a Fairy Tale World...
Bradford Smith needed to get rid of his scruffy image...
fast! And buying a week of feisty beauty Parris Hammond's
consulting services was the answer to his prayers. But would
the sassy socialite be able to turn this sexy, but stylistically chal-
lenged dud into the stud of her dreams?

#1747 THE LEAST LIKELY GROOM—Linda Goodnight
Clinging to a dream, injured bull rider Jett Garret would do *anything* to return to the circuit—and the pretty nurse he'd
hired was his ticket back to the danger he craved. But after
spending time with Becka Washburn and her young son,
Jett soon found himself thinking the real danger might
be losing this ready-made family.

#1748 THE TRUTH ABOUT PLAIN JANE—
Roxann Delaney
In a big curly wig and fake glasses, Meg Chastain had come to
Trey Brannigan's dude ranch to write the exposé that would
make her career. Meg knew the Triple B meant everything
to Trey...but she was out to prove that she could be
so much more....

#1749 LOVE CHRONICLES—Lissa Manley
Sunny Williams was on a mission—to convince oh-so-sexy
Connor Forbes that her holistic methods would enhance his
small-town medical practice. The dishy doctor had never
valued alternative medicine, but as Connor spent time with
the beautiful blonde, he began to discover that he might
want to make sweet Sunny his partner for good!

SRCNM1104